*Gabe ~~wished~~ ~~~~*
**Casey his secret.**

Are you an idiot? he raged at himself. She's the last person you should have told! It'll probably be on the ten o'clock news.

He shouldn't have trusted her. She was trouble with a capital *T*.

Yet for some inexplicable reason, he was drawn to her.

Why?

She was attractive, yes—but that wasn't it. Not that he wasn't sexually attracted to her, because he was. But there was something else, something more.

And it scared the daylights out of him.

Dear Reader,

Where's the best place to find love this holiday season? UNDER THE MISTLETOE! This month, Silhouette Romance brings you a special collection of stories filled with spirited romance and holiday cheer.

'Tis the season for Christmas wishes, and nine-year-old Danny Morgan has a tall order. He wants to reunite his divorced parents. Will FABULOUS FATHER Luke Morgan be able to win ex-wife Sherri Morgan's love—and fulfill his son's dreams? Find out in Carla Cassidy's heartwarming romance, *Anything for Danny*.

Helen R. Myers brings us a wonderful romance about the power of true love. *To Wed at Christmas* is David Shepherd and Harmony Martin's wish—though their feuding families struggle to keep them apart.

Linda Varner continues the trilogy, MR. RIGHT, INC. with *Believing in Miracles*. Falling in love again may be out of the question for single dad Andy Fulbright. But when he meets Honey Truman, *marriage* isn't....

Look for more love and cheer with a charming book from Toni Collins. *Miss Scrooge* may not have much Christmas spirit, but it's nothing that a holiday with sexy Gabe Wheeler can't cure. Lucinda Lambert is running from danger when she finds protection and love in the arms of *A Cowboy for Christmas*. Look for this emotional romance by Stella Bagwell. And Lynn Bulock rounds out the month with the delightful *Surprise Package*.

Wishing you a happy holiday and wonderful New Year!

Anne Canadeo
Senior Editor

Please address questions and book requests to:
Silhouette Reader Service
U.S.: 3010 Walden Ave., P.O. Box 1325, Buffalo, NY 14269
Canadian: P.O. Box 609, Fort Erie, Ont. L2A 5X3

# MISS SCROOGE

## Toni Collins

*Silhouette*
ROMANCE™
Published by Silhouette Books
America's Publisher of Contemporary Romance

For Mom...
who never seems to mind watching
the 1938 film version of *A Christmas Carol*
with me on Christmas Eve...
*every year*

 SILHOUETTE BOOKS

ISBN 0-373-19050-6

MISS SCROOGE

Copyright © 1994 by Toni Collins

**Books by Toni Collins**

Silhouette Romance

*Ms. Maxwell and Son* #664
*Letters from Home* #893
*Something Old* #941
*Miracle Dad* #1008
*Miss Scrooge* #1050

Silhouette Desire

*Immoral Support* #686

---

## *TONI COLLINS*

is a bestselling author of mainstream novels under her real name. She has worked in numerous occupations, all with one goal in mind: to one day realize her dream of being a full-time writer.

When Ms. Collins began writing for Silhouette Books, she felt a greater freedom with the category romance format, since she felt that she "could do things in these books that simply didn't fit" her mainsteam books.

Ms. Collins has traveled extensively and now lives in St. Louis with her son.

## Recipe for:
## CHRISTMAS JOY

$^1/_2$ cup hugs
4 tsp kisses
$^3/_4$ cup smiles
4 cups love
1 cup special holiday cheer
$^1/_2$ cup peace on earth
3 tsp Christmas spirits
2 cups goodwill toward men
1 sprig of mistletoe
1 medium-size bag Christmas snowflakes
(the regular kind won't do)

Mix hugs, kisses, smiles and love until consistent.
Blend in holiday cheer, peace on earth, Christmas
spirits and goodwill toward men. Use mixture to fill a
large, warm heart, where it can be stored for a lifetime
(never goes bad!). Serve as desired under mistletoe,
sprinkled liberally with special Christmas snowflakes.
Is especially good when accompanied by Christmas
carols and family get-togethers. Serves all.

# Chapter One

"Happy holidays, Casey!"

"Yeah, right." Casey Tucker, attractive except for the fact that she didn't smile very much, didn't look up from the notes she was reviewing. She told herself—and anyone else who dared to intrude—that she was going on the air in less than an hour and at this point was not ready. She would go over the notes a dozen times if necessary before airtime in order to be prepared. She would not tolerate any interruptions while she was doing this; she hadn't, after all, gotten to be one of the top TV newscasters in New York City by being slipshod or careless.

But Nina Blair was her producer, and the woman interrupted whenever she felt like it without fear of reprisal. "What have you got planned for Christmas?" she asked, knowing full well how much she was annoying Casey.

Casey shrugged, her attention still on her notes. "Nothing special," she answered absently. "Why do you ask?"

"*Why?*" Nina stared at her incredulously. "This is Christmas we're talking about, for crying out loud! You have *no* plans? Not even a family dinner?"

"I have no family," Casey said quietly. Not anymore, she was thinking.

"No one?"

"No one."

Nina frowned. Casey could guess what the other woman was thinking. Casey had only been at WRBC four months, so no one there knew very much about her personal life—but then, neither had the people at WATC, where she'd worked for almost ten years. She wanted it that way. She felt that if she was doing her job, she was under no particular obligation to share her private affairs with her colleagues.

Obsessive, Andy had once called her. More than once, actually. She was vividly remembering the last time.

"We're having a twenty-two-pound turkey—plenty there for one more," Nina was saying.

Casey shook her head. "Look, Nina, I really appreciate your concern, but—"

"It's more than concern, kiddo," Nina reassured her. "Joe and I really like you. So do the kids. We'd love to have you."

Casey shook his head again. "Thanks, but I don't think so," she said firmly.

"The door's always open if you change your mind," Nina promised.

"I won't. But thanks anyway."

Casey had no intention of spending the holidays with Nina or anyone else. It would, she knew from experience, only make matters worse.

Casey Tucker hated Christmas and all the other so-called "family" holidays—Thanksgiving, Easter, Mother's Day, Father's Day. They weren't happy occasions to her, just reminders of what she didn't have.

What she'd lost.

Family holidays made her think of the parents she'd lost as a child, of the husband she'd lost much more recently. Family holidays made her more acutely aware of her own loneliness—though she would never have admitted that to anyone but herself.

Never let 'em see you cry, she'd told herself.

She'd learned—the hard way—to keep her feelings to herself, not to let her emotions show. That way, she reasoned, she couldn't be hurt. Or at least it reduced the odds.

If she got too lonely, she could always buy a dog. Or a cat.

"Hey, Casey! Call on line two!" the WRBC receptionist yelled out, interrupting her thoughts.

"Got it." Casey reached for the phone. "Casey Tucker here."

"Ms. Tucker," the male voice on the other end of the line began, "my name is Gabe Wheeler. I'm director of the Guardian Angel Shelter—I work with the homeless and battered women and children."

Casey sighed heavily. This time of the year they were coming out of the woodwork, all of them with their hands out. "Look, Mr.—"

"Wheeler."

"Mr. Wheeler—if you're looking for donations—"

"Yes, I am, Ms. Tucker, but not money. Though we can always use that," he admitted. "What I'm looking for is a bit of your time."

"I'm afraid I don't understand."

"A story for your program. Airtime," he explained.

"I'm afraid—"

"I could give you enough stories to keep you on the air for a year," he said gravely, "and the shelter could use the publicity."

"I don't know." Just what I don't need, she thought. Dudley Do-Right of New York.

"At least think about it," he said, pressuring her.

"I will," she told him, willing to tell him anything to get rid of him. "I'll call you." Sure I will. "It's almost airtime. I really do have to go—"

"If you're going to call me back, won't you need my number?" he asked.

"What—oh, sure. Give it to me." She reached for a pen.

He did.

"When will you get back to me?" he wanted to know.

"Soon," she promised.

"By next week?"

"Definitely."

*  *  *

A brush-off, Gabe Wheeler thought, staring at the phone in his hand. Definitely a brush-off.

But he wasn't giving up. She'd agreed to at least consider his proposal. She'd promised to give some thought to giving the center the badly needed media coverage, and he was going to hold her to that. Gabe Wheeler was nothing if not tenacious.

The Guardian Angel Shelter needed help, now more than ever, and Gabe wasn't about to let it—or the people who depended upon it—down. He'd known, right from the start, that TV was the answer to his prayers. He'd chosen Casey Tucker for the craziest of reasons: because she had a kind face. He'd watched her on the news day after day, taking in her shiny blond hair, her big blue eyes and her warm, friendly smile, and he was convinced that, of all the newscasters he'd seen so far, she was his best bet. Until he spoke to her on the phone, that is. He found her surprisingly cold and unfeeling.

Maybe I've made a mistake, he thought.

He'd been so sure he could persuade her, if only he could get her to hear him out. But now...

"Hey, Gabe—you busy?"

He turned. The elderly man standing in the
doorway of his tiny, cluttered office was such a sad
sight, now as much as the first time Gabe had seen
him in the hospital. "What's up, Delbert?" he
asked, trying to inject a hopeful tone into his voice.

"Heard anything yet?" the old man wanted to
know.

Gabe shook his head. "Not yet, Del, but you
know we won't give up."

Delbert nodded. "I keep thinkin' that the longer
it takes, the less likely we are to find her."

"We're doing everything we can, Del."

The old man nodded again and shuffled off. His
limp's getting worse, Gabe observed silently. He
liked Delbert, genuinely liked him. Delbert Cramer had come to New York from Iowa three weeks
ago in search of his runaway granddaughter, an
eighteen-year-old who'd left home shortly after the
death of her mother. It had cost old Delbert every
dime he had to make the trip—and he'd been
mugged his first night in town. Gabe had met him
while Del was in the hospital and brought him back
to the center after he was released because he had
nowhere else to go and no money. He'd been looking for his granddaughter ever since, never even
considering giving up.

Just one example, Gabe thought, of how TV could help....

Another day like this, Casey thought as she got out of the taxi in front of her apartment building on the Upper West Side, and I'll be a candidate for early retirement.

She grumbled to herself all the way up in the elevator, still grumbling as she let herself into the apartment and kicked off her shoes. It was definitely the holiday season that was bothering her. All that holiday cheer—there was enough phony sugar in the air to give a guy a toothache! And the department stores—the crowds were unbearable! She tried not to shop at this time of the year if she didn't have to. And usually she didn't.

After all, she did no Christmas shopping of her own—no tree, no special dinner, no gifts. She had no one to buy gifts for.

Automatically her gaze went to two brass-framed photographs on the mantel. Her parents...so happy, so devoted to each other and to their only daughter. Casey blinked back a tear. Maybe things would be different now if they had lived. Maybe she wouldn't have married Andy. Maybe she wouldn't feel as she did. Maybe...

The photo next to that of her parents was of her husband, Andy Tucker. She still couldn't get used to the idea that he was gone, that he was never coming back. She still expected to see him walk through the door at any minute. She still thought of herself as being married. She tried to tell herself there was nothing abnormal about that.

After all, it had only been two years.

Why? she asked herself, as she had countless times over the past couple of years. Why did it have to be this way? What went wrong?

She turned her attention to the day's mail, unwilling to dwell on her pain any longer. Bills and junk mail—as usual. And a few Christmas cards, which she lumped in with the junk mail. She checked her answering machine. Nothing special, nothing urgent.

The story of my life, she thought.

She went into the kitchen, popping a frozen dinner into the microwave. She seldom cooked these days—it didn't make sense to even try. She wasn't such a hot cook to start with. She could only imagine what would happen if she tried to reduce a recipe to serve only one person.

Andy had always said he didn't marry her for her skill in the kitchen, which was a good thing, she recalled with bittersweet amusement. Yet he loved her. He told her he wanted to spend the rest of his life with her and he had—as little time as that had been.

It's not fair, she thought angrily. We didn't have enough time. Not nearly enough.

She turned on the TV. No matter which channel she flipped to, she found Christmas programming: *Miracle on 34th Street* . . . *Frosty the Snowman* . . . *A Christmas Carol*—the 1938 version—*How the Grinch Stole Christmas*.

That's me, Casey thought. The Grinch.

Or so her colleagues thought. They just didn't understand. No one did.

No one—at least no one she knew personally—understood the painful memories unearthed for her by the holidays, especially Christmas. No one understood that department store window displays and Christmas carolers and jolly men in Santa suits were, for her, just unpleasant reminders of her own loneliness and loss.

Her work had kept her going after Andy died. She'd put in long hours because she dreaded going home at night. While he was alive, he had dispelled the darkness she'd lived with before he came into her life. After he died, it was even worse. But her work had saved her. Ironically it was because of Andy that she became so successful. If it hadn't been for my loneliness, she told herself, I'd probably still be doing the entertainment news.

Then she remembered that she had always loved doing the entertainment news.


"Where're we going, Gabe?" Tim Rafferty wanted to know.

"It's a shortcut," Gabe told the boy. "After we're finished at the grocery store, I want you to take the groceries back while I run another errand, okay?"

"You bet."

Gabe didn't usually do the grocery shopping for the shelter. That job went to Tootie, a big, buxom Hispanic woman who ran her kitchen as if it were a military installation. Gabe only filled in when Tootie was otherwise occupied—as she was today, dealing with a gruff repairman and a highly temperamental refrigeration unit that had been around since Prohibition.

When Gabe did do the shopping, he always took Tim along. Tim was a big help—as he was forever telling Tootie, who insisted on shopping alone. Tim was twelve, a bright, outgoing boy in spite of the circumstances that had brought him to the shelter.

His mother had simply left him there six months ago. No note, no explanation, no nothing. Just deposited him on the doorstep and told him to go inside and tell them he needed help. Then she had disappeared, and no one had been able to find her. Gabe got him into school and got himself appointed his foster parent. In the beginning he'd hoped the woman's conscience would prompt her to return for her son. But she never did come back. As time passed, Gabe couldn't help growing attached to Tim, who was like a son to him. Even physically, there was a resemblance. Tim had the same build, the same thick brown hair, the same dark eyes, even the same smile. He could have been Gabe's son, and Gabe didn't want to give him up.

Gabe knew it was wrong, but that was how he felt.

"Can we get some cookies?" Tim was asking.

Gabe grinned. "Sure, why not?"

"Chocolate chip?"

"Is there any other kind?"

"And maybe some candy bars?"

"Hold it!" Gabe laughed. "I think we could get away with some stowaway cookies, but you know how Tootie gets when we don't stick to her list."

Tim made a face. "I can dream, can't I?"

"I know what you mean." Gabe chuckled. "Tell you what, why don't we stop somewhere cheap for lunch?"

Tim looked crestfallen.

"*And* a candy bar or two," Gabe added.

The boy brightened immediately. "All right!"

They cut through a construction site, one of many in the neighborhood. "Just what we need," Gabe grumbled. "Another high rise."

Tim shrugged. "Delbert says it's a good thing, that it means jobs."

"Sometimes it's good," Gabe said, nodding.

"But not this time?"

"Not this time," Gabe muttered eyeing the large sign on the fence surrounding the site. The Haynes Company. Gabe knew Ed Haynes well enough—too well, in fact—to believe for a minute that any Haynes project would ever mean anything good for anybody. What it did mean, most likely, was the lowest possible wages for his men, substandard materials and as much corner-cutting as old Ed Haynes could legally get away with. Haynes was fond of saying he got rich by taking chances. What he didn't say was that the chances he took were mostly with other people's lives.

Gabe was ashamed to admit that they were re-lated in any way—so he didn't.

"Gabe Wheeler, Ms. Tucker." He extended his hand. "We spoke about a week ago."

She regarded him with a blank look.

"On the phone."

Still no sign of recognition.

"The shelter," he offered helpfully. "The hu-man-interest story."

"Oh, yes." She nodded slowly. "The guardian angel."

"The Guardian Angel *Shelter,*" he corrected. She couldn't be more indifferent, he thought. She was more attractive on TV, but he guessed that was because on TV, she was almost always smiling.

"What can I do for you, Mr. Wheeler?"

"You promised to get back to me."

Another blank look.

Gabe wondered if she was having a bad day or if she was just that indifferent to his predicament. "When we talked last week, you promised to get back to me about doing a story on the shelter," he reminded her. "You never did."

"I'm sorry," she said, avoiding his eyes. "It's been a hectic week. It gets that way this time of year, unfortunately."

He took a seat even though she had not invited him to sit. "I think you could be a big help to the shelter if you'd do a story on us, Ms. Tucker," he told her. "We operate mainly on donations, but not all that many New Yorkers even know we exist. You could change that with just a few minutes of airtime."

She nodded. "What kind of story did you have in mind?" she asked.

He didn't hesitate to seize the opportunity to share his ideas with her. "You could do a little background on the shelter itself, then maybe feature some of the people we help."

"Give me examples."

"There's an old guy—came to New York a few weeks ago from the Midwest looking for his granddaughter," Gabe told her. "No sooner got here than he got mugged."

"Did he ever find his granddaughter?"

Gabe shook his head. "No—but we haven't given up."

"Tell me more." She seemed genuinely interested.

Thank God, Gabe thought without realizing the importance of such a thought for someone like him.

# Chapter Two

What have I gotten myself into? Casey wondered.

She thought about it after Gabe Wheeler had left the station. Why did he decide to pick on her, anyway? This wasn't even her kind of story. She normally did hard news—shootings, robberies, car jackings, street gangs, the stories her male colleagues all competed for. What made this man think she'd be interested in doing a story on a homeless shelter?

"Because it's Christmas," he'd told her. Little did he know.

She liked her station manager's reasons better.

"Ratings, Casey," Henry Parker had said. "Everyone will watch. People will care."

Casey gave him a wry smile. "This is New York...remember?"

He made a face. "That's just a stereotype and you know it."

She nodded slowly, and folded her arms across her chest, studying him for a long moment. "So," she started carefully, "you really think a segment—"

"Not just a segment," he said, shaking his head. "A series. One or two weeks' worth of segments. And yes—I think it could be a big ratings winner."

That, Casey thought now, was always the bottom line.

As her thoughts returned to the present, she told herself this wasn't going to be a problem. It wouldn't be the most hard-hitting assignment she'd ever had, certainly, but it wouldn't be a royal pain, either. She wasn't the type to let a sob story get to her. She'd never had a problem maintaining her professional objectivity, and she wouldn't have a problem with it now.

She'd done too good a job of shutting off her own feelings.

It was necessary, she'd told herself time and time again. She had to keep her distance emotionally, because if she let anyone get too close, if she let herself care, she'd be opening herself up to be hurt again.

And that was the one thing she simply could not risk. She looked at the snapshots in the collection frame on her desk. Happy photos, she thought sadly. Photos of happier times...of a happier Casey. Photos of a laughing child perched on her father's shoulders...a smiling young girl in gingham at her mother's side...a radiant bride on her wedding day, so happy and so much in love. It seemed to Casey that she was looking at photos of someone else.

Not her.

No, not me, she thought. That was another woman, another lifetime.

The child in those photos, the woman she became, was someone who had every reason to be happy. Until all of the reasons for her happiness were taken away.

Until everyone she'd ever loved died.

It was still very much on her mind when she left the TV station that evening and boarded the up-town bus, headed for home. The bus was crowded, so she had to stand for most of the ride. That wasn't easy, what with all the Christmas shoppers on board, most of whom were carrying bulging shopping bags filled beyond capacity with brightly colored, gift-wrapped packages. More than once, she was poked in the ribs or backside by sharp corners. She had to bite her tongue to keep from voicing her objections in a more explicit way. If they were going to buy so much in one trip, why couldn't they take taxis and leave mass transit to those who were making better use of their time? Casey mentally counted the number of seats occupied by packages or shopping bags and promptly decided it should be illegal.

I'm standing up—for this? she asked herself, more than a little annoyed.

It made her angry. Angry not only because she had to stand, but because it made her think, made her remember. And that was the last thing she wanted to do. More than anything, she wanted to forget. But she never could . . .

"When you get home tonight, Casey, we'll have the tree up," her mother had told her that fateful night as she was getting dressed to go caroling with her Sunday school group.

"I won't get to help decorate it?" Casey had
given her a crestfallen look.

Her mother had offered a prompt but condi-
tional surrender. "We'll save you some of the or-
naments to hang," she'd promised as she brushed
her daughter's hair.

But when Casey returned that night, there was
nothing left for her—no tree, no home, no family.
She remembered standing in the driveway, clinging
to the minister's wife, sobbing uncontrollably as she
tried not to look at the charred remains of what
had, only hours before, been their beautiful home.
Casey remembered feeling something brush against
her foot, looking down to see one lone Christmas
tree ornament lying in the gravel, untouched by the
fire.

She'd picked it up, holding it tightly as if it were
her last hope, a magical orb that could make everything all right again.

But it hadn't. Nothing had ever been right again
after that night.

That was her most vivid memory of a night she'd
spent the rest of her life trying to block out. That
Christmas Eve, so many year ago, had changed her
life drastically, changed it forever. Today, she
couldn't look at a Christmas tree or hear carolers

sing without seeing, mentally, that ornament lying at her feet, smelling the smoke as the firemen used their hoses to keep the flames from erupting again.

In a way, Casey felt as if she had died that night along with her parents. The most important part— the feeling part—had been lost forever.

"Out! Out! *Out!*" Tootie screamed.

The large Hispanic woman advanced on young Tim Rafferty menacingly, broom in hand. Knowing better than to tangle with her, especially on her own turf—specifically, her kitchen—he made tracks for the nearest door. His attention focused solely on making his escape, he didn't see Gabe coming toward him—and hit Gabe head-on.

"Hey, there!" Gabe laughed, grasping the boy's shoulders to steady him until he regained his balance. "What fire are you headed for?" he wanted to know.

"Tootie's on the warpath again!" Tim shrieked, obviously anxious to get as far away as fast as he could.

Gabe eyed him suspiciously. "What did you do to set her off?" he asked.

"Nothing, I swear!"

"Tim—"

"Okay, okay!" It was clear to Gabe that Tim was willing to do anything—even confess—to get Gabe to let him go. "Tootie's got some cookies in there... chocolate chocolate chip—"

"And you thought she probably wouldn't miss a few," Gabe concluded.

Tim nodded, too embarrassed to look Gabe in the eye.

Gabe laughed. "I'll let you in on a little secret, sport," he said in a conspiratorial tone. "Tootie always knows exactly what's in her kitchen, right down to the exact number of toothpicks at any given time."

Tim looked puzzled. "We don't use toothpicks, Gabe."

"You know what I mean."

Tim nodded. "Yeah... I guess so."

"The point is, even if you only took one, Tootie would know it," Gabe said.

"You think so?"

"I *know* so."

Tim frowned but said nothing.

"The point is, sport, that even if you *had* been able to get past Tootie, it would have been wrong," Gabe went on.

"It's just a cookie, Gabe."

"Today it might be 'just a cookie,' but tomorrow it could be two cookies, then a plate of cookies. Then, the entire cookie jar," Gabe said quietly.

"Don't be silly," the boy scoffed, then looked perplexed. "You're trying to tell me something, Gabe. What?"

"That honesty may indeed be the best policy."

"Always?"

"Always."

"Is it okay if I go now?"

"I suppose so."

Gabe watched, amused, as the boy hurried off. It was clear that he still expected Tootie to come bursting through the doors at any minute, brandishing whatever weapon she'd managed to lay her hands on. Tim hadn't been with them long enough to know that if Tootie really meant business, she'd have been on his tail the minute he came through the doors.

More likely, Gabe thought, she'd cooled off and went on about her business, content to have effectively barred him from her kitchen.

No, Tim hadn't been with them long. Just long enough for Gabe to have developed a strong emotional attachment to him. The more time Gabe spent with him, the more he missed being a father.

The more he missed his own son.

His own son…B.J. would be ten now, not much younger than Tim. He was a beautiful boy, a perfect combination of his mother and his father physically, bright and happy and full of life.

All too suddenly, that life had ended.

For Gabe, it had been a test of faith, one he had failed miserably. The day B.J. died, he'd stopped believing in anyone or anything. He hadn't been the same since that night five years ago.

Time *doesn't* heal all wounds, he thought now. Some wounds never heal.

He took his wallet from his hip pocket, opening it hesitantly. He kept no photographs of his son on display, either in his office or his living quarters, because it was too painful to have to look at them, day after day, knowing he was gone, that he would never be coming back to the father who loved him. But he'd never been able to remove the photos he'd always carried in his wallet. He seldom looked at them, unable to face his own pain, but he liked having them close to him.

Today, he looked.

He opened the photo compartment and slowly turned the small transparent pages, studying each photograph as if seeing them for the first time, as if he were trying to memorize the child's face.

As if he would—or could—ever forget.

His ex-wife was in some of the photos, too. She'd been so young when he married her, so surprisingly worldly. They had come together from two very different worlds, dooming their relationship right from the start. But they had loved each other and had believed—then—that love would be enough.

It might have been, he thought now, if B.J. had lived.


"So... what did the doctor have to say?" Gabe wanted to know.

"The baby could be born on Christmas Day—is that not wonderful?" Marie Rizzo, a small, dark, very pretty—and very pregnant—young woman stood in the doorway of Gabe's small office. She was, quite literally, glowing. "I knew my baby was going to be very special."

"Absolutely. Come, sit down," Gabe urged, indicating a chair for her. "You shouldn't be on your feet so much."

She nodded, seating herself somewhat awkwardly. "Thank you, Gabe. It is not so comfortable these days. My feet are puffy—most of the time I cannot wear shoes.''

"You're not getting enough rest." He scolded her lightly.

"You sound like the doctor—and my Joey."

"Where *is* Joey, anyway?" Gabe wanted to know.

Marie looked frustrated. "Where else? He is looking for work, as always," she said with a dismissive shrug. "He will never give up, no matter how many doors are slammed in his face."

"He'll find work, Marie." Gabe attempted to reassure her.

"I am beginning to wonder." She was silent for a long moment. "How can we possibly bring this baby into the world when we are unable to even give him a home?"

"I think it's a little late to reconsider bringing him—or her—into the world at this late date," Gabe remarked.

"It is a boy—I am sure of that."

"Okay—him," Gabe conceded. "And you do have a home—here—for as long as you need it."

She gave him a tired smile. "You are not much for obeying the rules, are you?" she asked.

He looked at her quite seriously. "Sometimes it's necessary to break the rules to get things done," he responded.

"I am not sure your employers would approve," she said with a twinkle of amusement in her dark eyes.

Gabe shrugged. "What they don't know won't get me fired," he said philosophically.

"You have been very kind to Joey and me," Marie began, "and do not think we do not appreciate it."

"But?"

"But I cannot be happy, I cannot feel secure, until we have a place of our own again," she admitted reluctantly.

"That's understandable," he said. "And it will happen, Marie, if you can just hang in there a while longer. Joey's a good worker, and he has the skills—"

"But people will not be quick to hire him because he has a record." She finished the sentence for him.

"Unfortunately that's true."

The phone rang then, interrupting their conversation. Gabe picked it up. "Guardian Angel Shelter. Wheeler here."

"Mr. Wheeler, this is Casey Tucker," said the husky female voice on the other end of the line.

"Ms. Tucker—I was beginning to think I'd been brushed off," he told her.

"Not at all," she assured him. "I needed an okay from my boss to do this kind of story."

"And?"

"He's very enthusiastic, Mr. Wheeler. He not only wants to do a segment, but he wants a whole series—profiling you and some of the people you've helped."

There was a long pause. "Some of our residents are more than willing to be profiled, Ms. Tucker," he told her, "but not me."

"But—"

"Not me, Ms. Tucker," he repeated for emphasis.

And he hung up.

What's he afraid of? Casey wondered.

She sat there at her desk, staring at the phone, trying to figure out what had just taken place.

And why.

Gabe Wheeler had just made it abundantly clear to her that he did not want to be profiled in her series, that he *would not* be profiled. She considered the possibility that he did not want to detract from the real purpose of the series—to call attention to those who really needed help—but journalistic instinct told her that there was more to it than that.

There might be a bigger story here than I thought, she told herself.

But she wouldn't be able to investigate Gabe Wheeler today, she decided after checking the time. She had to be at City Hall in ten minutes. Taking her bulky shoulder bag from the bottom drawer, she signaled her cameraman, Ben Hovis, en route to the rear exit, where the station vans were always parked. "Let's roll!" she called out, pushing the heavy door open.

"Right behind you, Casey!" came the response.

As they navigated the heavy crosstown traffic, Casey gave Ben directions on how she planned to do the interview and what she expected of him. Until it was over, she would shut everything else out, focusing only on the interview at hand. But afterward...afterward, it would be a different story.

Afterward, she would satisfy her curiosity about Mr. Gabriel Wheeler.

This was just what he *didn't* need.

When he'd gone to Casey Tucker seeking media coverage for the shelter, he'd had no intention of playing a role in the segment beyond that. The last thing he wanted or needed was to be on TV. Too much of the past—his past—could be dredged up. Too much he'd worked hard to bury, to keep buried.

No...Ms. Casey Tucker could just forget about putting him on TV.

"Those flyers you ordered are here, Gabe."

The young woman's voice cut through his thoughts. He looked up to see Wendy, a volunteer at the shelter, standing in the doorway, holding a large brown cardboard box. He nodded, rising to his feet to take it from her. "Thanks for picking them up, Wendy," he said.

"No problem," she assured him. "How soon do you want to get them out?"

"Yesterday." He took one of the flyers off the top of the stack and examined it carefully. It was a photograph of Delbert Cramer's granddaughter, along with her name, age and other relevant data. Above the photo, in large block letters: HAVE YOU SEEN THIS YOUNG WOMAN?

"Has Del seen any of this yet?" Wendy wanted to know.

Gabe nodded. "He helped me put it all together."

"Think it'll help?"

He shrugged. "I hope so. It can't hurt."

She looked at the flyer, too. "He must really love his granddaughter," she commented.

"Of course he does."

"I mean, look at all he's gone through to find her."

Gabe looked at her. "Wouldn't you, if you were in his place?"

Her response was a totally honest one. "I don't know what I would or wouldn't do."

"Well, I do," he said with certainty. "I'd move heaven and earth to get my child back." If only I could get my child back, he was thinking. If only I had that chance. A slim one's better than none at all.

"Hey, Gabe!" Tim poked his head around the corner. "You're wanted up front!"

Gabe waved him off. "It'll have to wait," he insisted.

"Can't," the boy said, shaking his head. "Somebody's here to see you."

"The police? The fire department?"

"A lady," Tim told him. "Says her name's Casey Tucker."

# Chapter Three

"Frankly, Mr. Wheeler, I don't understand why you don't want to appear on camera," Casey told him.

"You don't *have* to understand, Ms. Tucker," Gabe responded sharply. Not bothering to wait for her, he started off down the corridor toward the room where she would be taping her interviews.

"But you're an integral part of all of this," she insisted, hurrying to keep up with his long, quick stride. "Sort of the glue that holds everything together."

He stopped in his tracks, turning to face her. "Exactly—and when you've done a good job of putting things together, the glue doesn't show," he reminded her.

"All right, all right." She surrendered, raising a hand to silence him. "Have it your way."

"I intend to," he replied mirthlessly.

As she entered the room, she put down her bag and gestured to the cameraman trailing behind her to go ahead and set up his equipment. "Where do we start?" she asked. "Or should I ask with whom?"

He thought about it a moment. "With Joey and Marie, if they're around," he said.

"Yeah, I grew up here in New York—we both did," Joey Rizzo told Casey. He sat across from her, his very pregnant wife at his side, wringing his hands nervously.

"Don't either of you have any family, then, who would take you in, help you out?" Casey asked.

Gabe, standing just out of camera range, shook his head disapprovingly. He was beginning to wonder if he'd made a mistake. This woman seemed totally incapable of any semblance of compassion.

Joey shook his head. "Plenty of family, yeah, but nobody willing to help us in any way," he said quietly.

"Why is that?"

Marie spoke up. "Our families were dead set against us getting married, Ms. Tucker," she explained. "When we did, both sides—his and mine—wrote us off as if we no longer existed. Even when we had no home or food, they refused to even speak to us."

"My father had had it with me long before Marie and me got married," Joey interjected. "I'd gotten into a lot of trouble as a kid—"

"You mean with the law?" Casey asked.

He frowned. "Sometimes, yeah," he answered with a nod.

"What kind of trouble?" Casey wanted to know.

He gave a small shrug. "Shoplifting—always small stuff, like a lot of kids in our neighborhood did—and vandalism. At least that's what the cops called it. What it was, really, was a bunch of kids throwing rocks at an old building that was abandoned anyway," he said, remembering the past. "I got labeled a bad seed."

"That alone caused your father's attitude toward you?" Casey asked dubiously.

"No," Marie said, shaking her head sadly. "That happened when he was sent away."

"Sent away?"

"To juvenile."

"You mean juvenile detention?" Casey asked.

Marie nodded.

"What for?" Casey pursued.

Joey avoided Casey's eyes. "I was with a bunch of guys one night—Marie's brother was one of them—and two of them decided, without telling the rest of us, to hold up a liquor store in the Bronx," he said. "Because the rest of us were with them, we all got the same punishment."

"You did time, then," Casey concluded.

"Eighteen months," he admitted.

"In juvenile detention."

"Yeah."

"This is why it is so hard for Joey to find work now," Marie added. "He has a record, so most people are afraid to take a chance on him. To hire him."

"Does your brother have the same problem?" Casey wanted to know.

Marie shook her head. "My brother is dead, Ms. Tucker," she said in a barely audible voice.

"Could you speak up, please, and look at the camera?" Casey directed.

"She said her brother's dead," Joey said crossly, taking his wife's hand. "Lorenzo was killed in a fight while at the center."

"I see."

Gabe, still watching from the sidelines, wondered what Casey Tucker's problem could be. Joey had just told her that Marie's kid brother had been killed and all she could manage in response was a tight, very cold, *I see.* No *I'm sorry,* no compassion, no kind of emotional response.

It's as if she has no soul, he thought, troubled by the implication.

"How many people do you usually keep here, Mr. Wheeler?" Casey inquired.

"This isn't a kennel, Ms. Tucker," he said tightly. "We don't *keep* anybody. We provide them with a place to stay and food to eat until they can get back on their feet."

"For as long as they need it?"

"I beg your pardon?"

"Do you have a set time limit?"

"For what?"

"How long an individual can stay."

He shook his head. "No, of course not."

"Must get pretty crowded."

"Sometimes, yes."

"I guess you have to turn some away, then."

He shook his head again. "We never turn any-one back onto the streets, Ms. Tucker," he told her. "If there's no possible way we can take them in, we'll find a shelter that can—but no one is ever left on the streets if they come to us for help."

Casey was silent for a moment. "If there's no set time limit as to how long someone could stay here, don't you have a problem with the lazy ones, the ones just looking for a free ride?" she asked. "Someone could just move in here and live off the shelter—"

He glared at her. "Where'd you learn to be so cynical?" he snapped.

"I'm a realist, Mr. Wheeler," she said sharply.

"I always thought I was," he said evenly, "but I never thought being a realist required a total loss of compassion."

Gabe made no attempt to stop her when she stalked off angrily, headed for the nearest fire exit.

I *have* made a mistake, he told himself. A *huge* mistake.

The man is an idealistic idiot, Casey fumed—but only to herself. With genuine interest she watched

the videotape of her interview with Joey and Marie
Rizzo. The young couple came off as being completely sincere. The viewers will love it, she thought
with satisfaction. Maybe I *will* get something out of
this—most likely just a promotion or a raise, she
figured. After all, according to Gabe Wheeler, she
didn't have a compassionate bone in her body.

If only I didn't have to deal with Gabe Wheeler.

Who does he think he is, anyway? she wondered, amazed by his gall. Where does he get off
talking to me like that?

And why am I letting him get to me?

She'd had to deal with men like him before, but
in the past they'd never been a problem. She'd always been able to handle them. Why, she asked
herself, was this one different? How had he managed to strike a nerve when no one else could?

"You've got a winner here," Nina told her.
"There won't be a dry eye within a fifty-mile ra-
dius."

"This is only the beginning," Casey told her.
"Wait'll you see some of the others."

Nina thought about it for a moment. "Know
what? We should set up a fund to help these people—you know, invite our viewers to send dona-

tions in to the station. Those things are always a smashing success.''

Casey laughed. "Not you, too!''

Nina looked confused. "Me too what?'' she wanted to know.

"You've been taken in!''

"Taken in?'' Nina still didn't understand.

"You've fallen for this sob story!''

"Who wouldn't?''

"*I* wouldn't!''

"Oh, Case—''

"They're probably not even telling true stories, Nina! He did time. He's not about to go out and get a job as long as Mr. Do-gooder Wheeler will put a roof over his head and food in his belly,'' Casey proclaimed.

"You heard what he said,'' Nina offered in Joey Rizzo's defense.

Casey nodded. "I heard it. I just didn't believe a word of it. How could the Rizzos be so happy or nice if what they say is true?''

"Oh, come on, Casey,'' Nina urged, appalled. "Anyone can make a mistake—and he's right, it *is* hard for someone with a record to find a job.''

"He was involved in a holdup.''

"Not willingly, according to him.

"In case you haven't noticed, that's what they all say," Casey said pointedly.

"I give up." Nina rose to her feet and started for the door. "Casey Tucker, you *are* impossible."

Casey Tucker is impossible, Gabe thought, frustrated.

This has been one colossal mistake. I should have gone to someone else.

"Hey, Gabe—got a minute?"

He looked up to see Wendy Wilkins standing in the doorway. "Sure," he said wearily. "What's up?"

"Those flyers we put out on old Delbert's granddaughter."

"What about them?"

"We've already started getting calls," she told him.

"That's good . . . isn't it?"

"Maybe."

"What's the problem?" he asked.

Wendy frowned. "I think most of the calls we're getting are cranks," she said.

"But you're not absolutely certain."

"Well, no."

Gabe drew in a deep breath. "We can't take any chances," he said. "We have to check out every lead."

"With a police escort, I hope."

He gave her a withering look. "Get real, Wendy."

"Too much to hope for, huh?"

"I would think so."

"Too bad."

"Have you checked out the half-way houses?"

"Sure—those were the first places we looked," Wendy assured him. "Is that lady reporter coming back anytime soon?"

"Probably." Unfortunately, he thought. My fault. I picked the wrong person for our story.


"My producer wants to ask our viewers to send in donations," Casey told Gabe.

It didn't surprise him at all that it had been someone else's idea rather than her own. She would never have come up with anything so generous and caring.

"I thought you'd be at least a little more enthusiastic," Casey was saying.

He looked at her as if seeing her for the first time. "I'm very pleased," he assured her. "Just a little surprised, that's all."

"The station's raised a great deal of money for worthwhile causes this way," Casey continued to explain.

He forced a smile he didn't really feel. "So I've heard."

"Is there a problem?" she asked.

He debated within himself, but only for a moment. "Yes, Ms. Tucker, there most definitely is a problem," he said finally.

"Would you care to tell me what it is?" she persisted.

He sighed heavily. "I don't like your attitude," he said bluntly.

She gave him an incredulous look. "I beg your pardon?"

"Just what I said. I don't like your attitude. I don't like the way you treated Joey and Marie during that so-called interview of yours."

"I'm a reporter, Mr. Wheeler. That's my job," she said in her own defense.

"This was supposed to be a human-interest story—not an inquisition," he reminded her.

"True," she said with a nod, "but either way, I still had a job to do."

"Was it part of your job to make those two kids feel like a couple of lazy, no-account bums just looking for a free lunch in between liquor store holdups?'' he demanded.

"He *does* have a record—'' Casey began, genuinely amazed by his attitude.

"The only thing that boy's guilty of is poor judgment!'' Gabe shot the words back at her. "He ran with the wrong crowd and he's paid his price for it—or don't *you* think he's paid enough?''

"I was only trying to establish the facts, the truth,'' she insisted.

"The *truth*, Ms. Tucker—or the truth as you want it to be?'' he asked coldly.

*"The truth!"*

"Let me make myself clear,'' he stated, the anger in his voice all too clear. "I will allow you to continue with the interviews, but I will *not* permit you to be abusive, verbally or otherwise, with these people—they've been through enough already!''

"Abusive?''

"Yes, Ms. Tucker, abusive.''

"Now, you listen to me, Mr. Wheeler—''

"No, Ms. Tucker, you listen to me. The next interview on your list is with an elderly man who came here to find his runaway granddaughter—and almost lost his life in the process. The last thing this man needs is a verbal assault by you.''

Her eyes narrowed. "Don't tell me how to conduct my interviews, Mr. Wheeler." Her tone held a warning note.

"I will when they take place at my shelter," he told her. "Make no mistake about it—pull another stunt like the one you pulled yesterday, and you'll be out of here so fast you won't know what hit you."

Casey hoped her nervousness didn't show.

It wasn't Gabe Wheeler's threat that was making her nervous—though that certainly hadn't done anything for her peace of mind—it was the interview itself. It was Delbert Cramer's story.

It hit a little too close to home as far as Casey was concerned.

"She was always a good girl." Tears welled up in Delbert's eyes as he spoke. "Never any trouble, according to her mama. She was a quiet girl, a good student. Shy. Makes me worry all the more, 'cause I don't think she can cope out there on her own, especially in a place like New York."

"Why would she have come here, Delbert?" Casey asked, surprised by the uncharacteristic softness in her own voice.

He shrugged. "I wish I knew."

"Could she have had friends here?"

"I suppose—but if she did, she never talked about them to anybody," he replied.

Casey said nothing, waiting for him to go on.

"There was a flood last year—did a lot of damage, left a lot of families without homes. Some of them moved away, but they were farmers. I doubt they'd come here."

"Where was your granddaughter living after the deaths of your daughter and son-in-law?"

"My son-in-law died when Cathy was a baby, Miss Tucker," Delbert said, correcting her. "He was in the military. My daughter raised Cathy and ran that farm by herself until she died six months ago."

"How did she die?" Casey wasn't sure she really wanted to know.

A fresh flow of tears came to his eyes. "Cancer," he said in a low, strained voice. "Bone cancer."

"I'm sorry." Casey meant it.

Delbert nodded. "Mary Ann could be so stubborn sometimes. She wouldn't let them take her legs off, said she might as well be dead. Couldn't do what had to be done around the farm without legs, she told the doctors. Never had any radiation or any other treatment, just did what she could to put

things in order in the time she had left." He paused.
"If I'd known..."

"You didn't know?"

He shook his head. "I didn't even know she was
sick until after she died. Nobody did. I found out
all of this from her doctor when I went there for the
funeral."

"She was never hospitalized?"

"No."

"Not even when she died?"

"No. I think that's what was hardest on Cathy."

"In what way?"

"Nobody saw either of them for weeks," Delbert recalled. "Then one night, Cathy called the
sheriff's office, said her mother had been in a lot of
pain but that she wasn't in pain at the time of the
call, that she didn't seem to be breathing. When
they got to the farm, Mary Ann was dead—and
Cathy was an emotional wreck."

"Where were you?"

"Florida," he answered. "I worked on a fishing
boat."

"When did Cathy run away?" Casey asked.
"How long after her mother's death?"

"She was already gone when I got there, just before the funeral. She'd been staying with a neigh-

bor, but she was so distressed—she blamed herself for what happened to her mother. She told the neighbor she should have called the doctor even when Mary Ann told her not to."

"Why do you think Mary Ann didn't want to be treated?"

"I wish I knew," he said. "I know she didn't want to be a burden to anybody. She didn't want to have to depend on anyone to do things for her. But mainly, I think she just wanted to be with Barry."

"Barry?"

"Barry Vincent. Her husband, Cathy's father. Mary Ann was never the same after he died."

"You don't think this could be a cry for help on Cathy's part?"

He shook his head. "I don't think she wants to be found."

"Maybe, then, that's why she came here," Casey suggested.

Delbert gave her a quizzical look.

"If she truly does not wish to be found, what better place to hide than New York?" Casey asked, speaking from experience.

"Maybe." He paused. "When the local police gave up on finding her, I went to the state police."

"And?"

"Nothing."

"Why do you think she came to New York?"

"I don't under—"

"What made you decide to look here?"

Delbert frowned. "I found some things in her room—pictures, newspaper clippings, things like that."

"About New York?"

"All of 'em."

"But she never talked about coming here?"

"Not to my knowledge," he said, shaking his head. "But she wouldn't have talked about it. That wasn't her way."

Casey paused for a moment to collect her thoughts. This was harder, much harder, than she'd expected it to be. "You've been through a great deal in your search for your granddaughter, Delbert," she said finally. "Would you care to elaborate...."

# Chapter Four

"I'm impressed," Gabe admitted.

Casey gave him a cool look. "By what?" she asked carefully.

"Your performance."

"What makes you think it was just a performance?" she asked.

He shook his head. "Well, if you'll excuse me for saying so, your approach to Delbert wasn't exactly in character," he noted.

She turned on him in anger. "And just how would *you* know what is or isn't in character for me?'' she demanded hotly. ''You don't even *know* me!''

Watching her walk away, Gabe was disturbed by what had just taken place between them. Her over-reaction was an indication that there was something more at issue here than just her annoyance with him.

For both of them.

He'd seen this sort of thing all too often in his former occupation not to be able to recognize the warning signs. Emotionally Casey Tucker was a woman in trouble—and somehow, it was tied to old Delbert and his granddaughter. The interview had reopened an old wound for her. He was sure of it.

*If I could get her to talk about it—* He stopped himself. She wasn't going to talk to him. He was probably the *last* person on the face of the earth she'd ever consider confiding in. They'd gotten off to the worst possible start, and it had all been downhill from there.

Downhill, he thought. The understatement of the year.

''How do you think it went?''

Wendy's words cut through his thoughts. ''What?'' he asked, because he hadn't been paying attention.

"How do you think it went?" she asked a second time.

He gave her a tired smile. "Better than I expected," he admitted.

"Was it just a rumor, or was she much easier on Del than she was on Joey and Marie?"

"No rumor," he assured her. "She was almost human."

Wendy laughed. "You really don't like her, do you?" she asked.

He was surprised by the question. "I don't dislike her," he insisted. *I'm not sure how I feel about her,* he was thinking.

Casey slept fitfully that night.

Talking to Delbert Cramer about his granddaughter had brought back the nightmares that had haunted her periodically for years, bringing to the surface everything she'd tried so hard to forget.

When she closed her eyes, she saw the farmhouse engulfed in flames. She saw Andy's plane exploding into flames on the tarmac.

She saw her own life going up in flames.

Literally.

Got to stop doing this, she told herself as she got out of bed and stumbled into the bathroom. Can't change the past.

Can't bring back the dead.

She switched on the light. Looking at her own reflection in the large mirror over the sink, she felt as though she were looking into the face of a stranger.

Who *are* you—really? she asked herself.

She was no longer sure.

Splashing cold water on her face, she returned to bed but not to sleep. She left the light on. Lying awake, staring up at the ceiling without really seeing it, she'd never felt more painfully alone.

"Nobody will be able to watch it without tears," Nina predicted again.

Casey wasn't listening. She was staring at the faces on the screen—her own and Delbert's—unnerved by the way her heart went out to the old man.

I don't want to care, she kept telling herself. I don't want to feel anything—for him or for anyone else.

Feeling meant hurting. She'd been hurt enough.

She was terrified of being hurt again. She couldn't risk that. She was certain she wouldn't survive another hurt. No...this was a chance she couldn't take. Not now, not ever.

"Casey?"

Nina's hand on her shoulder startled her, and she jerked. "What?"

Nina laughed. "I didn't mean to scare you. You were a million miles away, Casey!"

Casey shook her head. "Not quite that far," she said quietly. More like a thousand, she was thinking.

"Wherever you were, it certainly wasn't here," Nina said.

"I'm sorry," Casey said, shaking her head once more. "What were you saying?"

"I was saying that nobody will be able to watch this one without tears," Nina repeated. "Even the hardest heart will be moved by it."

Tell me about it, Casey thought miserably. "It's quite a story," she agreed.

"It's got to be the first time I've ever seen you moved by the plight of another human being," Nina commented.

Casey was silent for a long moment. "I always thought objectivity was a necessary trait in a good journalist," she said finally.

"Objectivity, yes, but a total lack of compassion makes people nervous," Nina said pointedly.

Casey fixed her gaze back on the monitor. "I didn't realize I was such a monster," she said.

"Monster?" Nina laughed at the thought. "You're not a monster, honey!"

"What would you call me, then, if I'm so cold and unfeeling?" she asked.

"I'd call you someone who's trying very hard—too hard, maybe—to keep a safe distance from other people," Nina said truthfully. "I don't know why. I wish I did. But whatever the reason, you are."

"Very perceptive, Dr. Freud," Casey said, forcing a lightness into her voice that she didn't really feel.

She wished Nina—and everyone else—would just leave it alone.

"Look, I didn't mean to offend you when I said—"

Casey cut Gabe off with a dismissive wave of her hand. "It's nothing," she said quickly, almost too quickly. "Let's just forget about it, okay?"

"I don't think so."

She looked surprised. "I beg your pardon?"

He pursed his lips thoughtfully. "I get the feeling I've struck a nerve," he said.

"If you did," she said evenly, avoiding his eyes, "it's my problem, not yours."

"I've been told I'm a good listener," he offered.

Her smile was cold. "I'll just bet you are."

"Can't hurt."

"Sorry. You may be a great listener, but unless I'm in front of a camera, I'm not a good talker," she told him.

"If you change your mind—"

"I won't," she reassured him. "Now...who will I be talking with today?"

Gabe made a few suggestions, realizing she wasn't about to discuss herself or her problems any further. At least not with him.

"We got some calls right after the broadcast last night," he told her. "We think a couple of them might be legitimate."

"Someone's seen Cathy?" Casey asked hopefully.

"It's possible."

"Delbert must be thrilled."

Gabe's smile was weary. "Del's had too many false alarms to get excited anymore," he said. "He'll get excited when he's face-to-face with his granddaughter again."

Casey nodded, understanding completely the hopelessness the elderly man must have felt all these months. Still, he had the chance. He had hope.

Casey wished she had as much.

Can't think about that now, she mentally commanded herself. Can't let myself think about that. Got to focus...keep my mind on the interviews.

Got to stop living in the past.


"It's amazing that they can be so cheerful," Casey said to Gabe as they watched some of the shelter's residents decorate a large Christmas tree.

He looked at her, genuinely surprised by her statement. "Why do you say that?" he asked.

"They have no reason to be cheerful—"

"What makes you think they don't?" he challenged.

"Oh, come now," she responded. "It should be obvious, even to you, Mr. Wheeler. They have no homes, no jobs, no means of taking care of themselves or their children."

"But they *do* have each other, Ms. Tucker—and they have those of us who care enough to reach out to them," he reminded her. "Most of all, they have hope, and they have faith."

"Faith!" Casey snorted. "Fat lot of good faith will do them with no roof over their heads and no food in their bellies!"

He gave her a knowing smile. "You might be surprised," he told her. "Don't knock faith till you've tried it."

"What makes you think I haven't?"

He raised an eyebrow. "A surgeon can tell if you've had an operation or not, can't he?"

She looked confused. "Yes, of course. But what has one to do with the other?"

He hesitated, debating whether or not to be the first to open up. "I was once, briefly, an ordained minister," he finally revealed. "In college, I majored in clinical psychology—you might say I'm an expert in crises of faith of all types."

"And you think I'm losing faith," Casey concluded.

His concern was sincere. "I think whatever faith you may have had was lost a long time ago," he told her.

She stiffened. "You also took courses in mind reading, did you?" she asked coldly.

He drew in a deep breath. "I feel sorry for you, Casey," he said softly, for the first time using her given name.

She turned away from him abruptly. "*You* feel sorry for *me?*" she asked in a strained voice. "You feel sorry for me—that's absurd!"

"Not absurd at all," he said, shaking his head. "I recognize your pain because I've been there myself."

"Right."

"You've lost someone."

"What makes you say that?" She looked like a frightened deer caught in the glare of an oncoming car's headlights.

"I can see your need to keep everyone at arm's length," he said simply. "Something I did myself for many years."

"Really? Why?"

He paused. "Maybe I'll tell you about it someday."

"Right. You want me to open up to you, but all you're willing to tell me is that maybe, just maybe, you'll tell me your story one day."

"Let's just say I want to make sure it doesn't turn up on TV."

"Let's just play it safe on both sides and not say anything," she suggested.

He was still thinking about it after she had gone. For a while, he'd managed to successfully cut himself off from the outside world—emotionally—the way she was trying to do. Only she *wasn't* succeeding.

In reaching out to Casey Tucker, what would *he* be risking?

* * *

"He's a royal pain," Casey insisted.

"But a very good-looking one, Case," Nina said pointedly.

"He used to be an ordained minister," Casey said, stuffing some papers into a soft-sided brief-case.

"You're kidding!"

Casey shook her head. "I got it straight from the horse's mouth," she declared.

"Wow." Nina stared at her in amazement. "I shouldn't have stopped going to Sunday school."

Casey smiled knowingly. "Not exactly what you'd expect a preacher to look like, right?"

"Heck no," Nina said, nodding her agreement. "Unless you count the priest in *The Thorn Birds*."

"That's fiction," Casey stated.

"But what fiction!" Nina let out a low whistle of appreciation.

"I think he wants to save my soul," Casey said.

Nina looked deadly serious. "Doesn't he know you don't have one?" she asked.

Casey didn't take the bait. "Apparently not."

"Maybe you should let him try anyway," Nina suggested.

*"Whaaaaat!"*

Nina gave an offhanded shrug. "He'd be fighting a losing battle, of course, but what better way to get to know each other?"

Casey gave her a stern look. "What makes you think I *want* to get to know him—or let him get to know me, for that matter?"

Nina raised an eyebrow. "You could do a lot worse," she said bluntly.

Casey snatched up her bag and headed for the door. "Thanks a lot, Nina," she said as she departed, but she couldn't stop herself from thinking about Gabe.

She couldn't risk getting to know him. She'd only talked to him a few times—and those few times had invariably ended in arguments. He was the last person she could—or would even want to—confide in. What made him think she'd talk to him?

A double whammy, she thought miserably. An ex-preacher with a background in psychology. Just what I don't need.

She couldn't imagine herself discussing her deepest pain with a man she barely knew. It would be like going to a shrink. She'd never been able to understand how anyone could open up to a total stranger, someone they knew nothing about. And maybe Gabe was better left as just that—a stranger. Then she'd never have to tell him anything about herself. Because if she did open up to him, he might just use that intimate information against her.

She was nobody's fool. And never would be.

## Chapter Five

Gabe was up all night.

He wondered if he'd made a mistake in telling Casey Tucker anything about his past. She was a reporter, after all, a TV newscaster. And the last thing he needed or wanted was to call attention to himself.

Why did he feel such a need to reach out to her? Why her, of all people?

But that wasn't what was keeping him awake—at least not directly.

He was thinking about his own pain, his own loss. Dwelling on it, actually. How long had it been

now? In his heart, it still felt like yesterday. The
pain was every bit as unbearable as it had been the
day his young son was taken from him. How many
times in the course of his religious training had he
been told that all things happen for a reason, that
God's will had to be accepted? Pretty simplistic, he
thought . . . but he didn't believe it for a moment.

What possible reason could there be for the death
of a small child? he wondered now. What purpose
could be served by such a tragic loss? What was
there to be gained from it? How could anyone possibly benefit from it?

"It is God's will." Those words still echoed
through his mind. "We must not question God's
will."

Gabe had not only questioned it, but he had also
raged at it. He'd cursed God, denounced his faith
and turned his back on all he believed in and held
sacred.

He'd nearly destroyed himself.

Yet no matter how angry he had become, how
self-destructive, he had realized that the Man Up-
stairs had not given up on him.


"We have definitely gotten off to a bad start,"
Casey admitted somewhat uneasily.

Gabe nodded. "An understatement if ever I've heard one," he agreed. "But perhaps we could attempt a fresh start?"

She gave a little laugh. "You mean like an armed truce?" she asked.

He laughed, too. "A most appropriate comparison," he said. "But for now, I suppose it's the best we can possibly hope for."

"I think you may be right." She paused. "I've decided to take you up on your offer."

"Offer?"

"When you first came to me about doing this, you suggested I actually work here, get a feel for what life in a shelter is really like," she reminded him.

"I don't believe that's exactly what I said—"

"I'd like to bring my cameraman along," she continued to say. "It will be like a videotaped journal. Day by day, hour by hour—give my viewers a firsthand, up-close look."

He was about to reject her plan, but reconsidered. Aloud, he said, "You just might have something here."

"It was your idea," she reminded him.

Maybe, but he certainly didn't remember it. "Right."

"And don't forget, we're asking for donations."

"How could I forget? We need money desperately." But mentally he was still trying to figure out why he'd agreed to this. The only thing he could think of that would be worse than having her here for a few hours each day was having her all day, every day. They got along like Yankees and Confederates!

"Do you get any kind of state or federal aid?" she asked.

He shook his head. "This is a private operation."

"Corporation owned?"

"No, it's just what I said. It's privately owned."

"By one person or a group?"

"One person. And a lot of donations."

"Just donations?"

"That's about it."

"Then the person who actually owns it must be quite wealthy," she concluded.

"No, not really."

"You know who this person is, then."

"Of course."

"Name?"

"I can't tell you that."

"May I ask why?"

"It's really quite simple. Our benefactor prefers to remain anonymous," he told her.

"That's odd," she said with a peculiar look on her face.

"Not really. Some people do desire privacy, Ms. Tucker," he said pointedly.

"Ms. Tucker?" she asked. "Last night it was Casey—and you did say you wanted to make a fresh start."

"Right," he said with a nod. "Casey."

Resigning himself to the idea of her "working" there, he made some suggestions as to what duties she might assume as an unofficial member of the Guardian Angel's staff. Then they made the rounds of the facilities again. Finally Casey decided to ask the question that had been nagging her since their last meeting.

"You said you used to be an ordained minister," she began, somewhat hesitantly.

He frowned. "That's right."

"You're no longer a minister?"

"No, I'm not."

"I'm afraid I don't understand."

He raised an eyebrow. "What part don't you understand?" he asked.

"Well...how can you no longer be a minister?"

"Look around you," he told her. "I have no church, no parishioners. Haven't for several years now. What kind of a minister does that make me?"

"But once a minister is ordained, isn't he always a minister, no matter what?" she asked, clearly confused.

"Technically, yes."

"Technically?"

"In the eyes of the church, I might still officially be a minister, Casey—but in my heart, I divorced God a long time ago."

"Divorced Him?"

He nodded.

"Right. On what grounds?"

"Irreconcilable differences."

She'd thought he was putting her on.

He meant it, though. In the ways that really counted, he *had* "divorced" himself from God and the church. Now, Casey found herself wondering what could have happened to him to have so totally destroyed his faith.

Had he been telling the truth? she asked herself now. Could he have experienced the same pain and loss she had? Could he understand her feelings or lack thereof?

Could she risk it?

Did she even want to?

She'd convinced herself she was better off the way she was, isolating herself emotionally from the rest of the world. It was the only way, wasn't it, to keep from being hurt again?

Yes, she thought now, but is it the way I want to spend the rest of my life?

She was no longer sure.


He wished he hadn't told her.

What good could it possibly do? Gabe asked himself now. Casey Tucker was one of those people you looked at and just knew she was never going to change. She liked being the way she was, living the way she did. She was far too selfish, too ambitious, to want to share her life with anyone else. She probably didn't even know the meaning of the word compromise.

And he'd opened up to her.

Are you an idiot or are you an idiot? he raged at himself. She's the last person you should have told! It'll probably be on the ten o'clock news before the week is over.

He shouldn't have trusted her. He shouldn't have trusted her at all. She was trouble with a capital *T*.

Yet for some inexplicable reason, he was drawn to her.

Why?

She was attractive, yes—but that wasn't it. Not that he wasn't sexually attracted to her, because he was. But there was something else, something more.

And it scared the daylights out of him.

Whatever his problem was, he seems to have dealt with it.

She thought about it. He'd said he had experienced the same kind of pain and loss she had. Or at least he believed he had. He said it had destroyed his faith.

Maybe it had. But he certainly didn't seem scarred by it now.

If anything, he seemed too giving, too caring for his own good. Hardly the behavior of a man who had been deeply hurt. He seemed to be looking at the world through those proverbial rose-colored glasses. The attitude of a minister secure in his faith, yes, but not one who had admitted to having "divorced" himself from God. Not one who claimed to have suffered a loss of faith.

A mass of contradictions, she thought, intrigued.

I can't tell her, he decided.

I've told her too much already.

Why did he think she would understand? What, exactly, was it about her that made him so sure she'd been there, that she had known the kind of deep emotional pain he had?

Was it Fate that had brought them together? *All things happen for a reason...all things happen for a reason...all things happen for a reason.* The words echoed through his mind. He hadn't been able to accept that belief after B.J.'s death. He couldn't believe there could have been a good reason for his child's death. He still didn't. But *had* he and Casey Tucker been brought together for a specific reason? Was that why he'd chosen her when he decided to approach the TV stations? He didn't understand.

"Tell me," he pleaded, gazing skyward. "Is this the big game plan for me? Am I supposed to somehow save Casey from herself?"

Nina's right, Casey thought as she entered the shelter and caught sight of Gabe, who was giving instructions to members of his staff. He really *is* an attractive man.

She wondered if he dated.

Not that it really mattered to her. She was just curious. That was all. Trying to figure out what made Gabe Wheeler tick was like trying to put together a thousand-piece jigsaw puzzle with at least a hundred pieces missing.

Make that nine hundred pieces missing, she thought, mildly amused.

"Casey!" He waved when he saw her.

She waved back. "Where do I start?" she wanted to know.

"Let's go to my office," he said as she approached.

"Let me guess. I'm going to be your secretary," she said lightly.

He made a face. "*I'm* my secretary," he responded. "There's not enough in the budget for me to have a regular, paid secretary."

Casey had the feeling there wasn't enough for much of anything in the budget—yet she'd never heard him complain. Not being able to afford whatever she needed to keep things running smoothly would have made her nuts.

But he didn't complain. At least not where he might be overheard.

"We need to talk," he was saying.

She smiled. "Sounds serious."

"It is."

He ushered her into his small office and gestured her to sit down. She looked up at him expectantly. "What have I done now?" she wanted to know.

"It's not what you've done—it's what I think you might do," he said seriously.

"Meaning exactly what?"

"What I told you last night—"

"You mean about you being a minister?"

"Former minister," he said, correcting her.

She nodded. "Former minister."

"I told you that in confidence. It's not for publication," he said, clarifying his position.

"You didn't tell me it was off-the-record."

"I'm telling you now."

"Don't you think it would add a dimension to the story—"

"Whether it will add anything or not, I don't want it used," he insisted.

"I thought you were willing to do whatever was necessary to help these people."

His jaw tightened visibly. "I don't think it would be that much help."

Casey thought carefully before she spoke again. "What are you running away from?" she asked.

"What makes you think I'm running from anything?"

She felt oddly sympathetic toward him. "I know a runner when I see one." And to herself she added, It takes one to know one.

"Sorry to disappoint you," he said, "but you're way off base."

"Am I?" She wasn't convinced.

"Okay, okay." He chuckled. "Suppose you tell me. What am I running from?"

She was flustered. "How am I supposed to know?"

He gave an offhanded shrug. "It's your theory. Haven't you covered all the possible angles?"

"I don't know why you're running, but I know you are," she insisted stubbornly.

"I don't think you should broadcast it until you can prove it—do you?" he asked.

That made her angry. "Unfortunately, no," she admitted. "But as soon as I can, you get to be a cover story."

He smiled. "I don't think your bosses will find my story interesting enough to put me in the spotlight," he told her.

"Maybe, maybe not."

She was fuming when she left his office. He was taunting her! No wonder he's no longer a minister, she thought angrily. And because of that, she was more determined than ever to find out what it was he was so determined to hide.

You might as well tell her. She's going to find out anyway.

Gabe now knew she wasn't going to let up on him. She wasn't going to just forget about it, forget what he'd told her. If I hadn't made such a big deal of it, if I hadn't told her I'd broken with the church, maybe she would have ignored it. It's only a big deal to her because I don't want her to use it.

This is what I get for being a so-called Good Samaritan. I try to help her, and she wants to lay me bare for the world—or the population of New York City, at least—to see.

Some of us never learn.

Maybe I should have just told her and hoped she'd have the decency to keep a lid on it.

Casey Tucker? Who am I trying to kid?

In another life, she probably knew Charles Dickens. She was probably a real inspiration to him. Right down to the "bah humbug."

But he had the strong feeling that that was just a front, that she wasn't really the coldhearted witch she tried to make everyone think she was.

On the other hand, he thought, if she isn't, she's one terrific actress.

He looked skyward. "Okay, okay. I'm doing the best I can. But it's not going to be easy."


"We seem to bring out the worst in each other," Casey commented.

"Maybe we're too much alike," Gabe suggested.

Casey gave him a quizzical look. "What makes you say we're alike?" she asked. "From where I sit, we're not alike in any way, shape or form."

"I think we're both more emotionally vulnerable than we'd like to be," he told her. "I think we both have things in our pasts we'd like to forget."

"Why would you think I'm trying to forget something?"

"I think you try very hard not to care, which would suggest you're afraid to care," he said. "But Delbert got to you. It wasn't an act, was it? Your compassion for him was real, wasn't it?"

"Of course it was! I'm not that inhuman!"

"No, you're not. You may be more human than you'd like to be."

"I don't think I want to get into this—" she began.

"I'm not surprised," he said. "You have to talk to someone."

"Not necessarily."

"You'll never get over it if you keep it all bottled up within yourself," he warned.

"I won't get over it anyway," she said miserably.

## Chapter Six

"I blocked a lot of it out," Casey admitted the next day. "There's so much about that night that I don't remember. The clearest image I have of that night is standing in the driveway in front of the house—the firemen were still putting out the fire when the preacher's wife brought me home—looking at the house, what was left of it, and watching the coroner's people take my parents away."

Gabe reached out and took her hand in his. "I know how much this must hurt."

"How?" she asked. "*How* do you know?"

He frowned. "Because I've been there."

She looked at him questioningly. "You lost your parents, too?"

He shook his head. "My son."

"You have a son?"

"Had," he amended. "He's dead."

"I'm sorry," she said softly.

"Yeah, thanks."

"What happened to him?"

"Sudden Infant Death Syndrome—SIDS."

She looked at him, unable to conceal her sympathy. "Oh, Gabe—" she began, unable to get the words out.

"He was a perfect little boy, perfect in every way—or so it seemed," Gabe went on to explain. "He'd just had a checkup a few days before he died—the pediatrician said he was the picture of health. I'd been at the church late, and a baby-sitter was watching B.J. When I came home, the baby-sitter had left, and Lisa was asleep. So I went to look in on B.J. to kiss him goodnight, and I found him dead."

"It must have been devastating," Casey said feebly.

"To put it mildly."

"You were married, then."

"Yeah."

"Where's your wife now?"

"Ex-wife," he said quietly. "We divorced right after B.J. died."

"I can imagine that losing a child would put a great deal of stress on a marriage," she said.

He nodded. "If the marriage is a good one, a loss like ours usually brings a couple closer together. In a marriage that's already pulling apart at the seams, it can be the final blow."

She forced a smile. "Is that a professional opinion?" she asked.

"Professional?"

"You said your background is in clinical psychology."

"I said I was majoring in psychology when I decided to enter the ministry," he said, correcting her. "I'm not a therapist."

"That's not what I meant," she said quickly. "In either profession, there's a lot of counseling." Why on earth were they talking about this? Was it a way of avoiding the painful truths?

"I suppose."

"Where's your wife—ex-wife—now?" Casey asked.

He shrugged. "Europe." He paused. "She blamed me for B.J.'s death even more than I blamed myself. Her father sent her there to 'get over' me. As if there was anything left to get over.''

"I take it your in-laws are pretty well-off financially, then.''

"My father-in-law is,'' Gabe said, pacing the floor nervously. "Lisa's mother died when she was a little girl. I guess that's why she was so close to Daddy, why she couldn't see him for what he really was.''

"Meaning?''

He turned to face her. "Lisa's father is Ed Haynes.''

Casey couldn't hide her surprise. "Oh, I see.''

"I doubt I have to tell you about Ed Haynes.''

She shook her head. "I've lived in New York long enough to have heard all of the stories.'' She paused momentarily. "How much of it is true?''

"*All* of it—and more,'' he assured her.

"The two of you didn't get along,'' Casey concluded.

"That's like saying Pearl Harbor was a Sunday school picnic,'' he responded with a hollow laugh. "Old Ed Haynes was the most unethical, unscrupulous man I'd ever met—but he thought of himself as the cream of society. An inner-city minister wasn't good enough for his daughter, no matter how *she* felt."

"A snob," Casey commented.

"Yeah. He had somebody picked out for Lisa. Somebody he felt was 'right' for her—right position, right financial status, right attitude."

"In other words, someone just like Daddy," Casey said, guessing.

"Bingo."

"So he never accepted the marriage?"

"He never stopped trying to break us up," Gabe recalled. "Even after B.J. was born, he was always after Lisa to leave me, to bring the baby home—to his home—where his grandson could have the kind of life he felt he deserved."

"Sounds like Ed Haynes," Casey said, nodding.

"After B.J. died, Lisa was an emotional wreck," he reflected. "Ed talked her into coming home— just for a while, he said. Just until she was back to normal. She shouldn't be alone. There would be people there to look after her. She went along with him. She couldn't think for herself at that time, so it was easy for Haynes to persuade her."

"And she never came back."

He shook his head. "No, she didn't."

* * *

He's still carrying a torch for his ex-wife, Casey concluded.

It was obvious. The way he looked when he talked about her, the pain in his voice, the sadness. He still cared deeply for Lisa. After all they'd been through, all he'd suffered, and the way Lisa blamed him for the death of their son, how had he stood it?

He missed his wife as much as Casey missed Andy.

She still loved her husband, still missed him. So why did she feel so disappointed that he still seemed to have such deep feelings for his ex-wife?

You're not making sense, Tucker, she told herself.

"How's it going?"

Casey looked up to see Nina approaching. "I wish he'd pick on someone else," Casey confessed.

Nina gave her a quizzical look.

"It's been anything but fun."

"In what way?"

"First, there was no getting along with him," Casey began with a heavy sigh. "That was bad enough. But even now that we have a truce, he still brings out the worst in me."

"How so?"

"He makes me think."

Nina gave her a wicked smile. "That's not what he'd make me do," she confided.

"Nina!"

"He's very sexy—"

"Really, Nina."

"Don't tell me you haven't noticed."

"Yes, I've noticed he's a very attractive man," Casey conceded. "If you like that type."

"Who doesn't?"

"Any woman who sets her cap for him is going to be sorely disappointed," Casey said, busying herself with the videotapes she'd been viewing when Nina came in.

"What makes you say that?" Nina asked.

"He's still got it bad for his ex-wife."

"Ex-wife? I thought he was—"

"He was a minister, Nina, not a priest." Casey laughed. "They *can* get married, you know."

"So what about his ex-wife?" Nina asked, impatiently brushing Casey's comment aside.

"He was married to Ed Haynes's only daughter."

Nina couldn't hide her surprise. "Shady Eddie? His son-in-law is a minister?"

"Ex-son-in-law."

"Hard to believe."

Casey's smile was wry. "Having Ed Haynes for a father-in-law would be acceptable grounds for divorce, I would think."

"I wouldn't have married into that family to start with," Nina said with a mock shiver of distaste.

"I get the feeling Gabe is really hurting—"

"Gabe?" Nina smiled suggestively. "It's Gabe now, is it?" she asked.

"Don't make too much of that," Casey said quickly. "As I said, he's still in love with his ex-wife."

"He told you that?"

"He didn't have to."

Nina eyed her suspiciously. "Is it my imagination," she began, "or do you sound just a tad bit disappointed?"

"Me? You have to be kidding."

"Yeah, right." Nina didn't buy it.

Casey wasn't sure she bought it herself.

It was going to be a long night, Gabe decided.

It was two in the morning and as tired as he was, he couldn't get to sleep, no matter how hard he tried. He should have known, should have expected it. Talking about the past, about B.J. and Lisa, always had this effect on him.

Always.

He'd only been able to talk about his son a couple of times since the funeral. That had been part of the problem between him and Lisa. When she needed him most, he hadn't been there for her. At first she'd been hurt, then hurt gave way to anger and bitterness.

Not that he blamed her.

If he hadn't tried to divide his time so evenly between his church and his family, perhaps he would have been with B.J. and not with his parishioners. Perhaps he would have gotten to B.J. before it was too late. But B.J. had been with a baby-sitter. Gabe should have been with his son.

He wondered if Lisa was still living in Paris. The last he'd heard, she was about to remarry—to some French real estate developer. Ed Haynes no doubt approved wholeheartedly. Gabe wasn't bitter. He wished Lisa well, and hoped her new husband could make her happier than he'd been able to.

He couldn't even make himself happy.

Casey didn't sleep well that night.

Whenever she closed her eyes, all she saw was

fire. Flames, out of control, shooting upward into the darkness, engulfing her very soul.

Fire . . . fire . . . fire.

He was wrong, she thought. Talking about it didn't help. It only made it worse.

He'd reopened a wound that had never really healed. That would probably never heal.

She hadn't yet told him about Andy. She wasn't sure she ever would. She still had mixed feelings about having told him about her parents, about having shown him her vulnerability. Even now, she wasn't quite sure what it was about him that had finally made her open up.

And that made her more than a little nervous.

She got out of bed and went to her dressing table. In the top drawer was a small object wrapped in a silk scarf. She took it out as carefully as if she were lifting a baby from its crib. She unwrapped it with the same meticulous care. Within the protective folds of the scarf was a small, smooth round globe, brilliant blue in color, untouched in spite of what it had survived.

It was the Christmas tree ornament she'd found in the driveway that night, the night of the fire, so many years ago.

\* \* \*

"It is nothing. False labor, that is all," Marie insisted.

"Are you sure?" Casey asked dubiously.

"Yes," Marie said with a nod. "I have had it before. It is different from real labor because the pains are irregular. The doctor at the clinic tells me in real labor the pains are even, regular. Always the same number of minutes apart. Not five, then ten, then seven, as this is now."

"Yeah? How many children has he given birth to?" Casey wanted to know.

"*She.*" Marie said with a suppressed smile. "And she has seven of her own."

Casey didn't miss a beat. "Where did she ever find time to go to medical school?"

Gabe came into the room then. "What's wrong?" he asked.

"Marie has been having pains," Casey announced. "I think she should see a doctor."

"As I have already told Miss Tucker, I am sure it is just false labor," Marie protested.

"She's probably right, Casey," Gabe said, shaking his head but unable not to smile. "Nothing to worry about." He was still amazed at the change in Casey over the past few days. He thought it hard to reconcile the woman who tended Marie like a midwife now with the same cold, unfeeling reporter who had ripped Marie and her husband apart on camera.

He liked the change.

Aloud he asked, "Where's Joey?"

Marie frowned. "Still looking for work and finding nothing," she said dismally.

"Because of his record," Casey concluded.

Marie nodded.

Casey thought about it for a moment. "Let me talk to my station manager," she started to say. "We could use a driver. It doesn't pay much, but—"

Marie was genuinely surprised. "You would do that for Joey and me?"

"Sure—well, we *could* use somebody...though it really doesn't pay very well."

"That is all right," Marie said quickly. "Joey will take it, no matter how little it pays. It is a job, and that is all that matters right now to us."

Gabe smiled. He was starting to believe in miracles again. "Casey, could I talk to you for a minute?"

"Sure."

"Privately?"

"Oh...right." Casey stood up. "Lead the way."

"That was a wonderful thing you just did," Gabe told Casey once they were alone in his office.

"Don't praise me until he's got the job," Casey said, seating herself. "It's still up to my bosses."

"Regardless of the outcome, the concern and compassion you've shown Marie and Joey is, well, it's remarkable."

"You mean because I was so inhuman when I first came here?" Casey asked.

He looked at her. "You were never inhuman, Casey. You just made a monumental effort to conceal your humanity, that's all."

"An open heart gets broken," she told him.

"And a closed heart dies a slow and painful death."

"Speaking from experience?"

"I think we've both had experience in that area," he said tightly.

"You mentioned that your ex-wife is in Europe—"

"Paris," he answered. "She lives there now."

"How long has it been since you've seen her?" Casey was genuinely interested.

"Almost five years."

"I guess you must miss her a lot."

He turned to face her. "Why would you think that?" he asked.

She shrugged. "She is your wife."

"Was."

"Was," Casey repeated, nodding slowly.

"Lisa and I have been divorced for several years now. She's made a new life for herself in France, and I've made one for myself here."

"You never think about her anymore?"

"Of course I *think* about her from time to time," he said irritably. "She was my wife. We had a child together. Whatever went wrong between us, we had some very deep feelings for each other. That doesn't just stop one day because the marriage fails." He paused. "Where is this line of questioning headed?"

"I'm just curious, that's all."

"Why do I get the distinct feeling there's more to it than that, then?"

She pursed her lips thoughtfully. "Maybe you're overly sensitive about it because the existing feelings you have for Lisa are stronger than you're willing to admit. Even to yourself."

"Or maybe your interest is more than just simple curiosity," he suggested uneasily.

"Such as?"

"A story for your TV program."

She looked at him as though he'd slapped her. "I have no intention of using any of this on TV," she said angrily. "I was just concerned, that's all."

"Look, I—" he began.

"These discussions between us—that's exactly what they're going to remain. Between us. Private, off-the-record."

Gabe smiled. "Okay, okay. I apologize." And he meant it. This time, he believed her.

This time, he *trusted* her.

## Chapter Seven

"Can you meet me at the corner of Broadway and West 72nd Street?" Casey spoke excitedly into the telephone. "I've got a lead on Cathy Vincent."

"Are you sure it's not just another crank call?" Gabe asked, having been roused from a sound sleep by her call.

"I suppose it could be, but it sure sounded legit."

Gabe wondered if the caller hadn't sounded legitimate to Casey simply because she *wanted* it to be. He was bothered by Casey's apparently growing fixation with finding Delbert's granddaughter.

He wanted to find Cathy, too, but he was worried about Casey because he knew how strongly it was tied to her own loss.

"Where are you now?" he asked.

"At the station. On my way out," she said impatiently.

"You're not on foot, are you?"

"Of course not."

"You have a car, then."

"No. I'm taking the subway."

"Casey—"

"Have you ever tried to park in that part of town?" Casey asked, annoyed.

"Have you ever been on foot there at night?" he countered.

"I've been a lot of places at night that weren't considered too safe," she snapped back at him. "Now, Wheeler, are you with me or not?"

What choice did he have. "I'll be there in fifteen minutes, twenty tops."

"I'll see you there."

"Wait a minute—" He paused as the receiver clicked in his ear. He was going to ask her exactly where she would be. I guess I'll just have to find her, he thought as he got out of bed and hastily began to dress.

* * *

All right, Casey...where are you?

This place is busier than I expected—at least busier than I expected it to be at one in the morning, Gabe thought as he stood at the entrance to the subway station at Broadway and West 72nd Street. If she's taking the subway, though, she'll have to come through here. No chance of missing her.

Unless, of course, she's already here.

After half an hour he started to worry. Casey wouldn't be late. Punctuality was practically her middle name. By her own admission she hated tardiness.

Could she have arrived early? Impatient as she was, determined as she was to find Cathy Vincent, she might very well have. Had she met with the caller and gone off to look for Cathy?

Was she all right?

He decided he'd better start looking for her.

He checked out every restaurant and shop still open at that hour. Not only had she not been in any of those places, but no one who *had* been had seen her. He stopped long enough to call the police. When he told them who he was looking for, they just laughed and said she was probably off chasing

a story, that he should call them back if she was still
missing in twenty-four hours.

A lot of good that did, he thought irritably as he
hung up and set off on foot again.

He finally found her when he decided to check an
alley behind a restaurant on Broadway. He could
hear her moaning and went to investigate. She was
huddled near a Dumpster, clutching the upper part
of her right arm. "Casey?" Gabe asked, not sure
in the darkness that it was really her.

"Gabe," she gasped. "Help me...."

Only when he got closer did he see the blood.
"What happened?" he asked as he dropped to his
knees beside her. There was a small, but deep-
looking cut on her arm.

"I got here a little early. He was waiting at the
subway station," she said as he pried her hand off
her arm so he could get a better look at the wound.
"He told me he'd take me to Cathy."

"But instead, he brought you here," Gabe concluded, tearing the sleeve of her blouse away from
the wound.

She nodded, biting her lower lip in pain. "When
we got here, he pulled a knife on me," she said.
"He took my purse and my watch."

"You should have waited until I got here," he said, reprimanding her.

"Why?" she asked. "So he could mug both of us?"

"He would never have gotten us into this alley if I had been here."

"Right. You would have been smart enough not to go with him—unlike me."

"That's not what I meant at all," he said as he attempted to dress the wound. "Did he stab you before or after he robbed you?"

"Neither," she said testily. "He got me when I tried to scratch his eyes out."

"You tried to fight him?"

"Of course I did!"

"That was a stupid thing to do."

"You'll have to excuse me," she snapped back at him. "I seem to be doing a lot of stupid things these days—like trusting—trusting anyone! This is what happens when you start to care."

"Calm down, Casey, no one is faulting you," he told her. "I think the problem here is that you've lost your objectivity."

"Thanks a lot!"

"I wasn't insulting you. There's nothing wrong with caring so much about someone that you can't be objective about them." He paused. "This isn't going to work."

"What isn't?"

"This makeshift bandage. We have to get you to a hospital," he told her. "Can you stand?"

"I think so."

He helped her to her feet. "Can you walk?" he wanted to know.

"I don't know...I feel weak."

"Better not take any chances, then," he said. Scooping her up in his arms, he carried her to his truck.

"I have to go look at mug shots in the morning," Casey told Gabe as they entered her darkened apartment.

"What did the doctor in the ER have to say about that?" Gabe asked, concerned.

"Don't worry," she said quickly. "He said it would be all right as long as I didn't overdo it. I can't go to work. I have to take a couple of days off, until I regain my strength. But other than that—"

"I don't know if it's a good idea for you to stay here," he said, looking at the keys the super had given Casey to replace hers. This guy has your purse. He has your keys. And he knows where you live now."

"I'll be fine," she assured him. "There's a strong chain lock on my door, and this is a security building. Didn't you see the doorman when we came in? Or the security officers in the lobby?"

"I suppose," he said, unconvinced.

"You really don't have to worry."

"Maybe I should stay here—just for a couple of days, just until the police catch this guy." He paused, realizing how that must have sounded. "I could sleep on the couch."

Casey smiled knowingly. "You're welcome to stay, Gabe—if it will make you feel better."

"It would." He felt like an idiot.

She brought him a pillow and a blanket. "It's a lot more comfortable than it looks," she said, nodding toward the couch. And she felt a lot more comfortable than she was willing to admit, knowing that Gabe would be there.

He was awakened by the screams.

He was so startled by the screaming coming from the bedroom that he almost fell off the couch in his attempt to get up. He stumbled to the closed door and called her name. "Are you all right, Casey?" he called out to her.

When she didn't respond, he took a chance and went into the bedroom. She was sitting up in bed, sobbing uncontrollably. He sat down beside her and took her in his arms. "It's all right," he said softly, stroking her hair. "It was just a dream."

"I feel so stupid." She choked out the words.

"No reason to," he insisted. "It's a normal reaction to what you've been through tonight."

"I wasn't having nightmares about the attack."

"Oh?" He wasn't sure he had the right to ask what she *had* been dreaming about.

"I was dreaming about my husband," she said, as if reading his mind.

He couldn't hide his surprise. "Your... husband?" he asked.

She nodded.

"I didn't know you were married."

"I'm not anymore. That is, my husband is dead," she said, regaining her composure.

"I'm sorry."

She nodded again. "So am I."

"The nightmare...it was about his death, then?" he asked.

"Yes."

"How did he die?"

"He was an airline pilot," Casey said. "His plane went down."

"How long ago?" He wasn't sure he should ask, but she did seem to want to talk.

"Two years."

Two years of additional sorrow, Gabe thought. No wonder she was so reluctant to let anyone get close to her, let herself care about anyone.

"It was Christmastime," Casey was saying. "He was on his way home. He'd just called me from the city his flight was originating from. Said he had a surprise for me when he got home. I never got to know what it was—or see Andy again. The plane crashed—the cabin crew were all killed instantly, they tell me. Whatever was in the package burned to the point that it couldn't be identified."

She's still in mourning, Gabe thought. But why was that so troubling for him?

Because I care about her.

I care more for her than I want to.

Heaven help me.

Casey didn't know when she finally drifted off to sleep. She remembered only that Gabe was holding her, comforting her. How long had it been since anyone had held her, since she had *allowed* anyone to hold her? How long had it been since anyone had been able to give her any kind of comfort?

"Ah . . . you're awake."

She looked up as Gabe came into the room, carrying a tray. "What's this?"

"Breakfast—and you don't have to worry, I'm an experienced cook," he told her.

"Cooked at the shelter, did you?" she asked with mild amusement.

"As a matter of fact, I have, on occasion," he said as he positioned the tray across her lap. "I did all the cooking before we hired Tootie."

"And there was no loss of life?"

"My, aren't we in a good mood this morning?" he observed.

"Anything would have to be an improvement over last night," she said.

"I suppose you're right."

"From my point of view, anyway."

He looked down at the so far untouched tray. "Aren't you going to eat?" he asked.

"In a minute. We need to talk."

"I thought we talked ourselves to death last night," he said lightly.

She gave him a weary smile. "That's what we need to talk about."

"Sounds serious."

"I just wanted to thank you," she told him. "For being there for me—not just in that alley, but here as well. It's been a long time since I've been able to talk to anyone. About that, anyway.''

"I told you I was a good listener.''

"You are,'' she acknowledged with a nod. "I felt like you not only listened, but you cared.''

"I did—I mean, I do.''

She smiled. "I believe you do.''

"Is that so hard to believe?'' he wanted to know.

"For me, yes.''

"Why?''

"I can't explain it,'' she began with uncertainty. "Fear, maybe.''

"Fear?''

"Fear for you.''

"That doesn't make sense, Casey.''

"Think about it, Gabe,'' she said. "I loved my parents. They loved me. They died a horrible death in that fire. I loved Andy. He loved me. He died. Everyone I've ever loved has died a horrible, painful death.''

He hesitated momentarily. "Are you trying to tell me, in a roundabout way, that you're afraid to love me?''

"I'm trying to tell you that I *won't* love you.''

But she wouldn't say she *couldn't*.

*  *  *

"My brother is up from Miami," Tootie told Gabe. "He got a job driving a taxi. He would like to stay in New York, so who knows?"

"Now why would anyone who'd been living in Miami want to move to New York?" Delbert asked, finishing his coffee. "I was living in Florida before Mary Ann died, and if I didn't have to find Cathy, no way would I be here."

"In your case that's understandable, Del," Joey noted, "given your first impression of New York. But Marie and me, we both grew up here, and I can't imagine living anyplace else."

"I could," Marie said truthfully.

Her husband was unable to conceal his surprise. "You'd be willing to move away, to live in another city?"

She nodded. "If I thought we would be better off, that it would be better for our baby, yes, I would."

"What about your family?"

"You and the baby are my family now. I have no other," she said. "At least not as far as they are concerned."

Gabe came into the room then, not really paying any attention to the conversation in progress. His thoughts were with Casey and that conversation they'd had at her apartment. He understood what was going on inside her because he'd been there, he'd been scarred by the trauma of loss. What he didn't completely understand was what she was actually feeling.

She said she wouldn't love him.

She didn't say she couldn't—or that she didn't want to.

Now he had to ask himself what he felt for her. He'd felt something, right from the beginning, even when their relationship was an antagonistic one. He hadn't been sure exactly what that feeling was— even now he wasn't—but he was drawn to her, more so than he'd been with anyone since Lisa.

It could be love, he conceded.

But did he want it to be?

Casey had made it clear she was going to fight whatever feelings she had for him. She wasn't going to be a good candidate for a future long-term relationship.

Unless he could make her see that the deaths of her parents and her husband were not her fault, that they hadn't died because she loved them, because they loved her. Unless he could make her see that loving him wouldn't necessarily mean loving him to death.

What kind of guilt she must be feeling, he thought, troubled by the realization.

Could he possibly break down the wall she'd erected around her heart? Could he help Casey when he hadn't even been able to help himself?

Did he love her enough?

Do I love her? he asked himself.

"Hey, Gabe!"

Hearing his name, he turned to see Joey waving to him. "Yeah?"

"C'mon—join us."

"In a minute." He went to get himself a cup of coffee. It was cold, but he didn't really care. He'd probably drink it without tasting it anyway. He stirred in some sugar and a little powdered creamer, then took his cup and went to join the group. "What's this—a town meeting?" he asked, forcing a lightness into his voice that he didn't really feel.

"Right," Joey said with a chuckle. "We're debating the merits of New York compared to other cities with better climates and lower crime rates."

"Lower crime rates? Miami?" Delbert laughed aloud at the thought.

"You know what I mean," Joey insisted.

"Yeah—I know what you mean."

"Joey feels it would not be good to leave, even though he cannot get a job here and our families have washed their hands of us," Marie said solemnly.

"I said it would be very hard for me to leave— and it would be," Joey maintained somewhat irritably.

"I would go wherever I must," Marie disagreed.

"I don't much like it here," Delbert added. "I'm here 'cause I have to be. I'm here till I find Cathy."

"What do you think?" Marie wanted to know.

"I think everyone has to do what's best for them," Gabe said. He was thinking of Casey, wondering if she really knew what was best for her—at least when it came to affairs of the heart.

"Are you from New York, Gabe?" Delbert asked.

He shook his head. "I'm from Connecticut."

"What made you come here, then?" Marie asked.

"I was needed here."

They all gave him a quizzical look.

"What?" he asked, uncomfortable at the way they were looking at him.

"My work. The kind of work I do here," he explained. "This shelter needed me."

"Weren't you here before the shelter opened?" Joey asked.

His laugh was forced. "What is this, the Spanish Inquisition?" he wanted to know. "Why all the questions all at once?"

"Just curious, that's all."

"Well, it's been fun, but I can't stick around long enough for you guys to unearth all my deepest, darkest secrets," he told the group at large, rising to his feet again. "I have work to do."

"Gabe!"

Wendy was calling to him from the doorway. "What?" he responded.

"You've got a call. It's Casey Tucker."

## Chapter Eight

"I'm thinking of getting someone else to take over the assignment," Casey told Gabe.

"May I ask why?"

"I think it would be for the best."

"Best for who?" he wanted to know.

She was silent for a long moment. "All right, I admit it," she said finally. "It would be best for me."

"In what way?"

"Why all the questions?" she asked irritably. "What difference does it make?"

"Maybe none. Maybe a lot."

"You're talking in riddles, Wheeler. Cut to the chase, will you?"

"I think you're backing off because you're starting to feel something, and it scares the daylights out of you," he stated bluntly.

"Don't be silly. I learned to control my feelings a long time ago," she insisted.

"Maybe not as well as you think."

"What's that supposed to mean?"

"I think you want to control your feelings, that you'd like to think you can control them—but they tend to get away from you when you least expect it," he said.

"I see. You think I'm so much in love with you that I can't deal with it," she concluded.

"That's not what I said at all."

"Then what *are* you saying?" she demanded, annoyed.

"I'm saying only someone who really *has* cut all feeling from his or her life can successfully isolate themselves."

When she spoke again, there was contempt in her voice, but he knew it was all a front. "Is this the minister talking—or the shrink?" she wanted to know.

"This is the man talking," he said gently. "A man who cares very deeply for you."

"I can't do this," she said, her uneasiness obvious. "I have to go."

"No, Casey—wait."

"I can't. I have a call on the other line."

And she hung up.


She hoped no one could hear her crying.

As soon as she got off the phone, she'd locked herself in a stall in the ladies' room and gave her tears free reign. Why did he have to say that? Why did he have to tell her he cared about her?

Why did he have to be so perceptive?

He knew. He knew how she felt about him, hard as she'd fought it, hard as she'd tried to conceal it. Just as he'd known how deeply old Delbert and his granddaughter Cathy had touched her, even before he knew about her own past. He had the sensitivity of a cat. He could read people the way she read books.

His ability to read *her* was frightening.

Well, she thought, I definitely can't go back there now. I can only hope Nina and Henry will agree to replace me. But what do I tell them? I can't very well march into Henry's office and say, "You'll have to replace me on this one because I went and fell in love with the big jerk."

Dear God help me, I *am* in love with him.

What am I going to do?

What did I just say? Gabe asked himself, still staring at the phone.

I practically told her I loved her.

Sort of.

I told her I cared very deeply for her. Did she realize what I didn't even realize myself until just now?

Or did she think I knew how she felt about me and was trying to let her down gently by telling her I cared about her without using the word "love"?

Oh, no... that can't be it.

I have to be sure. I have to talk to her.

He dialed the station number. A woman's voice came on the line almost immediately. "Casey Tucker, please," he said.

"She's away from her office right now," the woman responded without hesitation. "Would you care to leave a message?"

He thought about that for a moment. If he left a message, she probably wouldn't return it. If he announced that he was going to drop by, she'd make sure she wasn't there when he arrived. No, leaving a message would definitely not be a good idea.

"No message," he said, and hung up.


"You want to what?"

"I want off the shelter story," Casey repeated, though she knew he'd heard every word she'd said the first time. "I think it would be better if someone else took over for me."

"Why?" Henry wanted to know.

Casey sighed heavily. She should have anticipated this. No way would Henry let her off a story midway without a very good reason. "Gabe Wheeler and I just don't get along," she said promptly. It wasn't exactly a lie. For most of their so-called working relationship they *hadn't* gotten along.

"That's not a good reason to quit."

"It is if the reporter in question—in this case, me—is supposed to be doing a human-interest story," she countered. "It's hard to be charitable toward someone you can't stand the sight of."

"It's not that bad, is it?"

"Just about."

He thought about it for a moment. "How much longer would you have to be there?" he asked finally.

"A week at the most. Probably less." Nina supplied the answer.

He shook his head. "It would be stupid to replace you at this late date," he said. "Sorry, Casey—you're just going to have to stick it out."

"But Henry—"

"It's not open for discussion."

"I see," Casey said with a heavy sigh of resignation. She turned on her heel and started out of the office.

Nina caught up with her halfway across the newsroom. "He's getting to you, isn't he?" she asked.

"Henry? No, I'm used to him."

"I'm not talking about Henry and you know it."

"No, I don't know."

"It's Gabe Wheeler, isn't it? He's finally gotten to you."

"No, he hasn't."

"Come *on,* Casey, admit it."

But she couldn't. She couldn't even admit it to herself.


"I tried to get someone to replace me on this story," Casey admitted.

Gabe looked at her, unable to hide his surprise. "Why?" he asked.

"I don't think I'm the right person for this."

He shook his head. "A couple of weeks ago, I would have agreed with you, but now, frankly, I can't imagine anyone else doing it."

She stopped what she was doing, which was putting canned goods into the large kitchen cabinets, and turned to face him. "Why is that, Gabe? What's changed?"

"You have," he said simply.

"In what way? Do I have a soul now, or what?" she wanted to know.

"Don't be so defensive," he said sharply. "You've always had a soul—but you've just been trying very hard to hide it."

She frowned but did not respond, turning her attention back to the task at hand.

"You've started to open up, Casey—to reach out to other people—and that scares you," he said. "That's why you want to retreat."

"Playing shrink again, are you?" she asked, trying to keep her voice deceptively light.

"You're afraid of being hurt again, aren't you?" he persisted.

"Is that so strange?" she asked. "Is it so odd to not want to be hurt?"

"It's not normal to just cut yourself off from the rest of the world," he said. "You can't avoid pain, Casey. It's a part of life."

"Did you feel that way when your son died?" she asked angrily.

He stared at her as if she'd slapped him. "No, I didn't," he admitted. "I felt a lot of anger, a lot of rage I couldn't control. I denounced my faith and left the church. I started to drink. I was caught driving drunk and knew I had hit rock bottom."

"Did you do time?" she asked.

He shook his head. "I got community service."

"Is that how you ended up here?" she asked.

He shook his head again. "I was working at another shelter, and I didn't like the way things were run there, so I bought this building and opened the Guardian Angel."

Casey couldn't hide her surprise. "*You* own the Guardian Angel?" she asked.

He nodded.

"Why the big secret?" she wanted to know. "Why didn't you want anyone to know you own it?"

"If you had a record like mine, would you want anyone to know you were in charge of a shelter for the homeless?" he questioned. "Would you trust somebody with a past like mine?"

"There's more to it than that, isn't there?" she guessed.

He was silent for a long moment. "Yes. I didn't want my former father-in-law to know what I was doing," he said. "I knew he'd do his best to cause trouble for me, and the people here would get the fallout. They don't need that."

Casey was thoughtful. "How did you learn to care about other people again?" she asked.

He smiled patiently. "It wasn't all that hard," he assured her.

"You were bitter, weren't you?"

"Very."

"Mistrustful?"

"Absolutely."

"Wasn't it hard for you to learn to open up again, as you put it, to let yourself care?"

"At first, yes," he confided. "It was the hardest thing I've ever done, aside from dealing with B.J.'s death. But the loneliness was just as painful as the loss."

"That's hard to believe."

"Think about it," he urged. "You've cut yourself off from anyone you might care too deeply about to avoid being hurt, right?"

She nodded.

"Are you happy the way you are, the way you've been?" he asked.

"No," she admitted reluctantly.

"Then think about what you're missing out on," he advised her.

"Have you *really* been able to pick up the pieces and go on as if your son never existed?" she asked dubiously.

"No, of course not," he said quickly. "Not a day passes that I don't think about him, mourn him. But love's a funny thing, Casey—the more you give, the more you *have* to give." He paused. "In many ways, Tim reminds me of B.J., makes me think about what my own son might be like now, had he lived."

"Is that why you're so fond of Tim?"

"That's part of it," he said honestly. "But I love Tim mostly for himself. I'd like him to be my son."

"You want to adopt him?"

"I would if I could."

"Why can't you?"

"Tim's mother just dropped him off here one day and vanished from the face of the earth," Gabe said regretfully. "For a long time, he was so withdrawn, he wouldn't even talk. I had to put in a lot of time with him. It broke my heart that anyone could do such a thing to her own child. I couldn't. I went to court and got myself appointed his legal guardian, but I was told that to adopt him, I would have to find his mother and get her permission."

"Even though she abandoned him?" Casey asked incredulously.

"That was my question," he said. "I was told that's the way the law works, for better or worse."

"But it doesn't make sense."

"No, it doesn't. But that's the way it is, so before I can adopt him, I have to find his mother. And that's easier said than done."

"Maybe I can help," she offered.

"How?"

"Television. I can fax her name and description—if you have a photo, that would be very helpful—to all of our affiliates. If anyone's seen her—"

"Yes, of course—but before we can do any of that, I have to talk to Tim, tell him what I'd like to do."

"You haven't talked to him about it yet?"

Gabe shook his head. "I wasn't sure how he'd feel about it."

"He seems to be crazy about you."

"I believe he cares for me, but he hasn't talked about his mother in a long time," Gabe said. "I don't know how he feels about her now. Does he expect her to come back, or what?"

"You've never had any trouble grilling me. Why haven't you talked to him about any of this?"

He shrugged. "I'm sure a part of him will always be holding out hope for his mother to come back. I'm not sure when the right time will come—if there's ever a 'right' time. I don't know."

"I've often wondered what a child of mine would have been like," Casey said then.

"Why didn't you and your husband have any?" he asked.

She struggled for a faint smile. "To be honest, I don't think my husband really wanted any," she confided. "Andy and I were drawn to each other because of the things we had in common—we were both orphans, for one thing. Andy grew up in foster homes, I with an aunt who never really wanted me. Neither of us ever really felt wanted. Never felt loved. Andy didn't remember his parents as I did, so he had no pleasant memories at all. He had nothing to draw from as a father, so he was ambivalent.''

''You loved him deeply, didn't you?'' Gabe asked softly.

Casey blinked back a tear. ''He used to say I was the only person in the world who had ever really loved him,'' she said in a barely audible voice.

''And he loved you.''

''Yes. I never felt more loved. He had so much to give, but he was so afraid to give it.''

''As you are.''

She avoided his eyes. ''Yes.''

''You don't have to be afraid, you know,'' he told her.

''I can't help it.'' She pulled away when he reached for her, but he wouldn't let her go.

''No, Casey—you have to stop running away from your feelings. Let the pain come. We can deal with it, you and I. Let me help you.''

She shook her head violently. ''No....''

''Go ahead, Casey—cry if you want to,'' he urged her. ''Let yourself *feel....* ''

She literally fell into his arms, sobbing uncontrollably. ''No...no...''

"It's all right, Casey," he said softly. "It's going to be all right."

When she raised her head and looked into his eyes, what he saw tore at his heart. Gently, very gently, he kissed her. "It's going to be all right," he promised. "In time, it will be all right."

## Chapter Nine

"I hope this one's on the up-and-up," Casey said, looking at Nina, who had approached her desk as she ended her telephone call and replaced the receiver.

"Let me guess. The Vincent girl?"

Casey nodded. "Another lead. I'm debating whether or not to follow up."

"Oh?" Nina raised an eyebrow questioningly.

"Every call we've had so far has been a crank."

"That may be true," Nina conceded with a half-hearted nod, "but you never know. This one could be the right one."

moved to join Andy at the table. "What did Vera want?" she asked, though she could guess. Obviously her ex-

Casey nodded, too. "That's what worries me."

Nina perched on the corner of the desk, pushing a stack of papers aside. "Listen, kiddo, you've got to learn to take chances," she advised. "Otherwise, you never know what you might miss out on."

"Are we talking about finding Cathy Vincent now—or something else?" Casey wanted to know.

"Wherever it applies." Nina reached out and patted her arm. "I just want to see you happy."

"Nina, when are you going to give up?"

"On your silver anniversary."

At that moment, Nina was paged, bringing their conversation to an abrupt end. As Casey watched her head off across the newsroom, she shook her head, more amused than annoyed, as she had once been, by Nina's attempts to sell her on the joys of matrimony.

These days, she wondered if the Ninas of the world could be right.

The phone rang then. She snatched it up. "Tucker here..."

"What's wrong with Joey?" Gabe wanted to know.

Marie shook her head. "He is like this every Christmas," she said darkly. "He will not admit it, but he misses his family."

"Has he tried to contact them?"

She shook her head again. "He has too much pride for that, I am afraid."

"He should make the first move if it means so much to him," Gabe advised. "Could be they feel the same way he does and have just as much pride."

Marie's smile was sad. "I am sure you are right about that."

"And it would be harder for an older person to bend," Gabe said pointedly.

"This I do not doubt."

"Talk to him, then."

Marie sighed heavily. "This I have done, Gabe," she told him. "I have talked and talked and talked, but I get nowhere. I have begun to wonder if I am not fighting a losing battle."

"Nothing is hopeless," Gabe insisted. And to himself he added, I know that from my own experience.

Casey was excited.

The call that came in as she was preparing to leave the station was the most convincing yet. She believed the caller, believed that this time she could be on the right track. This could really be it, she thought as her cameraman drove the station van across town to the Guardian Angel Shelter.

She had finally found Cathy Vincent. And on Christmas Eve.

There was a time the day would not have mattered—only getting the story. But Gabe Wheeler and the people he worked with at the shelter had changed all that for her. He—they—had made her open her heart, made her care.

Gabe had made her see that she, just maybe, could love again.

"Gabe, this is my brother, Juan."

Tootie beamed as she introduced the short, cheerful-looking man who had just arrived at the shelter. "It has been so long—too long."

"Have you ever been in the U.S. before, Juan?" Gabe asked.

"Once—but it was a very long time ago," Juan told him. "I lived and worked in Florida, in Miami. I worked on a fishing boat there."

"His visa expired," Tootie explained.

"I ran into much government red tape in trying to return to this country," Juan said, somewhat embarrassed. "It took a very long time."

"Where are you staying?" Wendy asked.

"I am with Tootie for the time being—until I can get a place of my own," Juan answered, putting an arm around his sister.

"Then you'll join us for Christmas dinner," Gabe said promptly.

"Here?"

"Of course."

"That would be very nice, of course, but I had planned to take her out to dinner, to thank her for all she has done to help me return to this country," Juan said. "If she is needed here, though—"

"No, no, no problem," Gabe assured him. "Tootie deserves a day off," he said quickly. "We'll manage."

"I can cook," Wendy volunteered.

Tootie looked at her oddly. "Gabe, you'd better put the paramedics on standby now," she warned.

"I *can* cook," Wendy declared.

"You may be able to cook, honey," Tootie began, "but can anybody *eat* it?"

"About as well as they can digest yours!" Wendy shot back.

"Calm down, you two!" Gabe intervened. "Where's your Christmas spirit?"

"Gone for the holidays!" Wendy responded. "Tell you what, Tootie—tonight, in the kitchen, we'll have a cook-off. Let everybody test both and give us a judgment."

"You're on, child." Tootie accepted the challenge.

Tim joined the group at that point with a message for Gabe. "Casey called from the station, said she's on her way," the boy told him. "Says she's got a lead on Del's granddaughter. She's sure this one's the real thing."

"That's great. Where is Del?"

"I thought he was in here with you guys."

"No." He turned. "Wendy, have you seen Del?"

She shook her head. "He left about an hour ago."

"If any of you see him, tell him Casey's coming for him—and tell him why, so he doesn't leave again," he instructed.

"Right."

"Okay."

"Will do."

"Got it."

He turned back to Tim. "I'd like to talk to you, sport," he said then.

"When?" Tim asked, obviously curious as to why Gabe wanted to have a talk.

"Tonight. After Casey comes for Del."

"Sounds important."

"It *is*—probably the most important talk we'll ever have."

"Am I in trouble?" Tim asked, suddenly worried.

Gabe smiled. "Not at all," he assured the boy. "This is a good kind of important, not a bad kind."

It was time for him to make some changes in his life, that was all. Changes that very definitely included Tim.

And Casey, if she was willing.

"Where's Marie?" Joey asked.

"She went to lie down for a while," Wendy told him.

"Is she all right?"

"Oh, I'm sure she is," Wendy said confidently. "Just a bad case of heartburn, she said."

"You made breakfast for her, didn't you, honey?" Tootie asked sweetly.

"You wish!"

"Hey, you two!" Gabe cut in. "Save your rivalry for the cook-off, all right?"

"I think I'll go check on Marie," Joey said, in spite of Wendy's reassurances.

"Casey's here!" Tim announced.

"Anybody seen Del?" Gabe wanted to know.

"I'll go check his room, see if he's back yet," Wendy volunteered.

Gabe nodded. He went to meet Casey. He needed to talk to her before he had his talk with Tim, before she left here tonight. This couldn't wait any longer.


"I've found her!" Casey greeted Gabe. "I've found Cathy!"

"You seem awfully sure this time," Gabe observed. "What makes you so certain this isn't just another crank call?"

"This woman—the person who called—knew things about Cathy only someone who knew her could be aware of," Casey explained. "She knew details of Cathy's life on the farm, details only Cathy could have revealed to her."

"I assume you're taking Del with you this time, then."

She nodded. "I was planning on it, yes."

"We're trying to find him now."

Casey looked surprised. "Trying to find him?" she asked. "He's not here?"

"He went out earlier. I'm not sure where—he usually doesn't stay away this long."

"Maybe we should look for him," Casey said.

"This is still pretty important to you, isn't it?" Gabe asked.

She nodded. "I wish I could explain why, but I can't even put it into words."

"It's all right," he told her. "I understand."

She studied him for a moment. "I think you really do," she said finally.

Just as he leaned forward to kiss her, the door opened. "Del's back. I told him Casey wants him to go with her," Tim said.

Gabe rolled his eyes upward. "Thanks, Tim," he said, groaning inwardly.

Casey laughed. "Maybe we should make an appointment to meet later—under the mistletoe," she suggested.

He shook his head. "We have to talk—now."

"What's so important it can't wait?" she wanted to know.

"Us—we're that important."

Before she could respond, the door opened again. This time, it was Joey. "Can you drive us to the hospital, Gabe?" he asked excitedly.

"The hospital?"

"Marie's in labor! She's having the baby!"

"It's all right, my angel," Joey told Marie, who was clearly experiencing a great deal of discomfort. "We'll be leaving as soon as Gabe gets the truck started and warmed up."

Casey looked on in silence. In spite of everything they had been through, all of the strikes against them, she envied Joey and Marie. She envied their love, their devotion to each other, their ability to endure the worst possible conditions because of their commitment to each other. She'd had so little of it in her own life that it had become all the more precious—and elusive—to her.

"We've got a problem." Gabe pulled off his gloves as he came inside. "The truck won't start."

"Let me take a look," Joey volunteered. "I can usually start even a temperamental car."

"He is very good with them," Marie agreed. "He worked for a while as a mechanic."

"Go ahead."

Tootie, who was tending Marie, nodded. "You have time. Her contractions are still pretty far apart. She won't have this baby real soon."

"I hope not," Marie said softly.

"I wish Juan had not left already, but he had to be at work," Tootie said. "He would see that you got to the hospital."

"Your brother got a job already?" Marie asked.

Tootie nodded. "He's drivin' a cab."

Gabe took Casey's arm. "About that talk—"

She gave him a wry smile. "Think we've got time, with all the chaos you have to deal with here tonight?" she asked.

"I'll *make* time."

"I doubt you'll be able to," she said, eyeing Marie.

"Let's go back to my office."

I've been doing a lot of thinking," he told her as soon as they were alone again. "About us, about what's happening between us."

"And?" she asked, not sure she really wanted to know what conclusion he had reached about the future of their relationship.

Wendy poked her head in the door then. "Del said to tell you he'll be ready to go in about ten minutes," she told Casey.

Casey nodded. "Tell him to meet me out in front," she said.

"Will do," Wendy replied.

"It's going to be a bit cramped," Casey told Gabe after Wendy had gone. "The studio's van has only two bucket seats, which means I'm going to have to sit on a couple of Ben's toolboxes."

Gabe looked frustrated. "I need a lock on that door," he decided promptly.

Casey laughed. "I'm sorry."

"For what?"

"I told Wendy where we were going and to let me know when Del was ready. We have to go soon. Ben has a family and would like to spend Christmas Eve with them."

"I'd like to spend Christmas with you," Gabe said then.

She smiled. "I'd like that, too."

"Would you, really?" he asked.

Her eyes met his. "I wouldn't say it if I didn't mean it," she responded.

"That's what we need to talk about—what you would like to be doing in the future," he said.

"Is this going to be multiple choice?" she asked, trying to hide her nervousness.

"I'm serious."

"That's what I'm afraid of."

"I can tell."

Tootie came to the door then. "Hey, Gabe—we got trouble," she told him.

"What now?" he asked, growing more frustrated by the minute.

"The truck won't start."

"I know that. Joey's working on it."

"No, he's come back. No way can he get it to run."

"Is he sure?"

"He says he tried everything, but it just won't go," Tootie said.

"Great," Gabe groaned as he started for the door. "How do we get Marie to the hospital?"

## Chapter Ten

"What's wrong with it?" Gabe wanted to know.

Joey shrugged. "I tried everything," he said. "I thought it might be the battery, but that checks out. I checked the fuel pump—that ain't it. I checked the alternator, you name it. It just won't start—but I can't find anything wrong with it."

"What are we going to do now?" Marie was justifiably worried.

"Don't worry, Marie—babies only arrive quickly on TV," Casey told her. "We'll have plenty of time to get to the hospital. In fact, I doubt if you'll actually give birth before morning, at the rate your labor is progressing."

"You are sure?"

"I'd bet real money on it."

"Couldn't we take her in your station van?" Joey asked.

Casey had already thought of that. "We could, but there are only two seats—bucket seats at that. The rest of the van is full of heavy equipment. I'm afraid she'll be very uncomfortable."

"If we have no other choice—"

"We can get a taxi," Gabe said then.

"On Christmas Eve?" Joey asked dubiously. "It will not be easy."

"Don't worry," Gabe said reassuringly. "We'll get her there in plenty of time."

"I could call Juan," Tootie offered.

"Yeah," Joey said, nodding. "Juan is a taxi driver. Yeah, call him."

Twenty minutes later, they were still waiting.

"Where is he?" Marie wondered aloud.

"I thought his dispatcher was going to radio him right away," Joey complained.

"That's what he told me," Tootie said, frustrated.

"I think we'd better start looking for an alternative means of getting there," Gabe said finally.

"Like what?" Joey wanted to know. "A bus? A donkey?"

Casey looked at Gabe, guessing that he didn't respond to Joey's sarcasm because he knew the young man was under a great deal of stress. She admired him for that. She would not have been so restrained.

At least she didn't think she would.

"I got your message. What's up?"

They all looked up to see Juan coming in, all smiles. "A surprise Christmas party, right?"

"You are half right," Tootie told him. "It is definitely a surprise, but we do not have time for a party now. Marie, as you can see, is about to have her baby."

He grinned. "Sure she is. Soon, didn't you say?"

"Tonight," Tootie told him. "She is in labor—and we need you to get her to the hospital."

"Tonight? Yeah, sure I'll take her—but traffic is heavy now," he worried aloud. "You sure we got time?"

"I think we have plenty of time to get to the hospital," Casey said confidently.

Marie looked up at her, puzzled. "You are not coming with us?"

Casey shook her head. "I don't think there's going to be room for all of us in Juan's cab," she said. "You'll need to lie down in the back seat—and Gabe will be up front with Juan and Joey. I'll meet you there." She turned to Gabe. "I don't have much time."

"Still taking Delbert to check out that lead?"

She nodded.

"Do you really think this one could be the right one?" he asked dubiously.

"Yes, I do." She smiled. "After all, you're the one who's always saying Christmas is a time for making miracles happen."

He smiled, too. "So I do," he admitted. "Are you starting to believe?"

"I'm starting to consider the possibility."

"For you, that's a real accomplishment."

"For Christmas, I asked Santa for a bit of humanity," she told him.

"For the record," he began, "you put in your request with the wrong department—but I suspect you'll get your wish anyway."

"That's comforting."

"I'll see you at the hospital, then?"

"Count on it."

He was about to kiss her when Delbert came into the room. "I'm ready to go, Casey—"

"Del?" Juan asked, surprised. "Del Cramer?"

"Juan?" Delbert was surprised, too. "Juan Menendez—what are you doing here?"

He hooted with laughter. "Tootie—she is my baby sister!"

"Baby!" Tootie snorted disapprovingly.

"I live here now, here in New York. How many years has it been?"

"Too many, you old scoundrel," Delbert told him. "We have a lot of catching up to do!"

"I agree—but unfortunately, not tonight," Juan said apologetically. "Tonight, I just take this lovely lady and her husband to the hospital to welcome their baby to the world."

Delbert nodded. "I'm here to find my granddaughter."

"Mary Ann's girl?"

Delbert frowned. "Yeah."

"Why do you have to look for her?" Juan asked as they all headed outside.

"It's a long story."

"Will you be here tomorrow?"

Delbert nodded.

"Me too. But in the afternoon I'm taking Tootie out for Christmas dinner. We can catch up later in the evening, I hope."

"Yeah."

Casey watched as Gabe and Joey helped Marie into the back of the cab. It had started to snow. Off in the distance, she could hear carolers singing what sounded like "Away in a Manger." For a moment, she felt something like magic stirring within the depths of her soul. But was it magic—or was it love?

She climbed into the back of the van and made a seat for herself atop two steel boxes. "Let's get this show on the road," she told her cameraman.

"You'd think people would stay home on Christmas Eve," Gabe said as he observed the unusually heavy crosstown traffic.

"There are a lot of parties tonight," Juan told him. "Very busy night in midtown."

Gabe didn't respond. He was thinking about what he'd planned for tonight, what he had intended to spend this evening doing. He was going to talk to Tim first, then he would have left him with Tootie and Wendy while he went to see Casey.

It would have been a special night, he thought now. How perfect it could have been.

He was going to ask Casey to marry him.

Do we have any chance for a future together?

As Ben negotiated the heavy traffic, Casey's mind was not where she believed it should have been. How long had she worked to make tonight happen, to reunite Delbert with his granddaughter? Gabe had more than once accused her of being obsessed with Delbert and Cathy Vincent. And if she were to be completely honest with herself, she had been. But now . . .

Now her mind was on something else.

Her thoughts were on Gabe, on the constantly changing nature of their relationship. She loved him. She did love him. There was a time, and not too long ago, she didn't believe she would ever be able to love anyone again.

And Gabriel Wheeler was the last man she would have expected to fall in love with.

So where does that leave me? she wondered.

"How far apart are the contractions now, Joey?" Gabe wanted to know.

"Every ten minutes." Joey attempted to soothe his wife. He'd gotten into the back seat with her, cradling her head in his lap, wiping her face with a damp cloth and holding her hand.

"The pain is terrible," she gasped.

"My mother used to tell me she gave birth to all of her children at home, with only a midwife, no doctors or medicines," Joey remembered. "I used to believe her, but now I suspect it was just a story."

"I hope I will not have to have this baby without a doctor or medications," she said in response.

"Lots of women do it every day when they can't get to the hospital in time," Gabe told her, hoping to calm her.

"I would not like to be one of them."

He smiled to himself. He wondered what Casey would be like in childbirth. Probably as impatient as always. She would not be one of those strong, tolerant women who could give birth in a taxicab or even at home. No, Casey would have to be in a hospital, complete with doctors and anesthetics.

He hoped he would have the opportunity to assist her in giving birth.

"Where is all this traffic coming from?" Casey asked, annoyed.

"It's Christmas Eve, Case," Ben reminded her. "You know, some people actually *do* celebrate the holidays."

"Yes, Ben, I am aware of that fact," Casey assured him in an irritated tone. "But shouldn't they be celebrating at home, with their families?"

"Has it ever occurred to you that some of them have to *drive* in order to get to their families?" Ben wanted to know.

"I hope this is her," Delbert said then, looking at the slip of paper on which Casey had written the address her contact had given her. "I can't bear the idea of Cathy being alone on Christmas."

"Don't worry, Del," Casey said, reaching forward to pat his hand reassuringly. "If she's out there, we'll find her."

She could only hope Cathy Vincent wanted to be found. Surely she did. Casey would have given anything if someone had cared enough about her to go to such lengths for her when her parents died.

"The snow—it is coming down heavier now," Juan said, worriedly, eyeing the heavy snowfall warily. "I hope we are not stuck here much longer."

Gabe twisted around to face the back seat as best he could. "How's she doing, Joey?"

"The contractions are still seven minutes apart," Joey said. "She is unable to get comfortable, even lying down."

"With any luck, it won't be much longer now." It had better not be, he was thinking. He didn't want to have to deliver her baby here, like this.

"How far is this hospital, anyway?" Juan wanted to know.

Joey looked surprised. "You're a cabdriver and you don't know where the—"

"I ain't been on the job long. I also ain't been in New York all that long," he admitted.

"That's okay, Juan," Gabe said. "I'll direct you."

At that point, the night was shattered by a deafening roar.

"What was that?" Casey asked, startled.

"Sounded like an explosion," Ben said, reaching for the CB radio. "Let's see what we can find out."

He switched it on, but there was so much static he couldn't hear anything. He tried another band. Same thing. He tried another and another, but the static was so bad, the best he could get was a very faint, broken transmission that was totally unintelligible.

"What's wrong with it?" Casey asked anxiously.

Ben shrugged. "It was working fine before we left the center."

In the distance, she could see lights flashing. "It may really have been an explosion," she said, suddenly concerned.

"If it is and the station can't reach us, we'll sure hear about it when we get back," Ben said grimly.

Casey just laughed. "Maybe we're lucky it's *not* working."

"Yeah."

She looked up at the sound of sirens wailing. "Maybe I'll walk up there, see what I can find out," she said.

"Streets might be slick with all this snow," Ben said, pointedly. "Sure you want to be out there trekking around in heels?"

"Don't worry about me," she told him. "I'm an old hand at this, remember?" She turned to Delbert. "Stay here with Ben. I won't be long."


"I'm gonna see if I can get an ambulance," Joey said, getting out of the car.

"Joey—" Marie reached out to him, frightened.

"It's okay, baby, I'll be right back," he promised. "I'm just going to find a phone and call the hospital. We could be stuck here all night."

As Gabe looked out the window, he saw Casey approaching from the rear, picking her way through what appeared to be a sea of automobiles. He waved to her. "Casey!" he called out to her. "Over here!"

She saw him and came forward, picking up her pace, even in the snow. "We've really got to stop meeting this way," she said lightly. "How's Marie doing?"

"She's doing just fine. Get in," he told her.

She shook her head. "I want to find out what's going on up there."

"In case you haven't noticed, it's snowing," he said.

"I've noticed," she assured him. "Beautiful, isn't it?"

He laughed. "I will never again look at another human being and say, 'He'll never change.'"

"Oh? And why is that?" she asked, starting to move on.

"A month ago, you wouldn't have thought this was beautiful at all," he reminded her. "All it would have been to you would be an inconvenience."

"You're right, it would have," she said with a nod. "But it's Christmas, Wheeler!"

Gabe smiled. "So it is."

"Is Marie really all right?" she asked then.

"She's hanging in there. Listen, why don't you stay here? Joey just went up that way—he'll be able to find out what's going on," Gabe said. "Besides, Marie could use a little female companionship right about now."

"Even though I've never had a baby myself?"

He shrugged. "You'll have to do."

"Thanks." She got into the cab. "How are you feeling, Marie?" she asked.

"The contractions are still seven minutes apart." She seemed out of breath.

"That's good. With any luck, we'll all be out of here long before the baby comes." She paused. "He's certainly going to have a remarkable entry into this world."

Gabe's eyes met hers in the darkness. "I have a feeling this is going to be a remarkable night in more ways than one," he said.

## Chapter Eleven

"What's the problem?" Casey wanted to know.

"That new building, the one under construction—part of the structure collapsed," Joey said, climbing back into the cab. "The police are up there, detouring traffic."

"But nothing's moving." Casey worried aloud.

"It's a mess, a big tie-up," Joey said. "Nobody's in the lanes they should be in, I don't think."

Marie moaned, gripped by another contraction.

"How far apart are they now?" Joey asked anxiously.

"Every seven minutes," Marie said breathlessly. "It cannot be much longer now."

"I hope it won't be too soon," Joey said, "at least not before we get to the hospital."

"That makes two of us." This was from Casey.

"I do not know if I can hold out that long," Marie told them.

"Where's Gabe?" Casey asked.

"He's talking to someone at the site."

"A man?"

Joey nodded.

Ed Haynes, Casey guessed, but didn't vocalize her suspicions.

"I don't think we're gonna be outta here anytime soon," Juan said then, craning his neck in an attempt to get a better look at the traffic situation ahead.

"Maybe we should look for a cop," Joey suggested. "They'll get Marie to the hospital."

"No!" Marie gripped his hand. "I'm not going without you!"

"You may have to, sweetheart," he told her. "We got to think about the baby now. He needs to be born in a hospital."

"I'm afraid, Joey," she admitted. "I do not think I can do this alone."

"We do what we have to do," he insisted.

Casey glanced backward, trying to see the station van, somewhere behind them in the traffic. Delbert was probably getting pretty impatient by now.

But there was nothing she could do about it at the moment.

Her pager beeped then. She was tempted to ignore it, but realized it could be important. "I'll be back," she said as she climbed out of the car.

"Where are you going?" Joey asked, openly alarmed.

"To look for a telephone. I'll be back."

Picking her way through a veritable sea of parked cars, she reached the sidewalk and started looking for a pay phone. She found one in the next block. "This had better be good," she muttered irritably as she dug into her bag for coins and dialed. Even if it *was* important, how could it possibly be any more so than what she was doing right now?

The call was from Nina. She returned it immediately. "It's Casey. What's up?" she wanted to know.

"Where are you?"

"You wouldn't believe it if I told you."

"Try me."

"All right," Casey said with a sigh. "A building collapsed and I'm stuck in the traffic jam of the century in a taxicab with a pregnant woman about to give birth, a former minister rediscovering his faith and two old friends who have been reunited after twenty-seven years—one of whom may find his missing granddaughter tonight, unless you're going to call me back to the station and throw a monkey wrench into our game plan."

"Relax. What I'm calling about will be very convenient for you."

"That's not possible. Nothing could be convenient for me right now."

"This is. I want you to cover the collapse of the Haynes project," Nina told her. "You do have Ben with you, don't you?"

"Sort of."

"Meaning exactly what?"

"I left the van to assist with Marie. She could have her baby any minute now," Casey explained hastily. "Ben's here somewhere in this mess, but—"

"Find him."

"You make this sound like a matter of life and death," Casey commented.

"It is. There are three men—the foreman and two of his men—trapped under the building," Nina told her, and hung up.

As she navigated through the traffic back to the car, Casey's mind was racing. Getting to Cathy Vincent would be impossible until the traffic cleared, so Casey figured she might as well do as Nina asked and cover the story. She just hoped she and Delbert got to Cathy in time.

"I have to find my cameraman," she told them when she reached the cab. "My boss needs me to cover this. I'll tell Del to stay with you, and if you can get out before I get back, go on to the hospital. I'll meet you there. Let Del know we'll go after Cathy as soon as we can."

Juan nodded, then turned back to Marie, trying to soothe her.

"The situation here is really bad. The foreman and two of his men are trapped in the wreckage," she told them.

Joey and Marie looked at each other, and Juan took each of their hands in his and squeezed.

"Casey, Joey's father is the foreman of the Haynes project," Marie said softly.

Casey looked at all of them, unable to speak.

*  *  *

"What's it going to take, Ed?" Gabe demanded angrily. "Do these men have to die before you realize you can't keep cutting corners to such dangerous extremes?"

"You'd like to blame everything on me," Haynes said contemptuously. "Including this."

"I'm not the only one who can—and will—blame this on you." Gabe shot the words back at him. "I think the Housing Authority will have quite a lot to say about your questionable business practices."

"I've been in business a long time, and they haven't intervened yet," Haynes responded haughtily.

"Sooner or later, your sins are bound to catch up with you."

Haynes laughed. "Once a preacher, always a preacher, eh?"

"I wasn't speaking as a minister," Gabe said pointedly. "Just someone who places a higher value on human life than you apparently do."

"Right. Too bad you didn't feel that way when my daughter left you in charge of my grandson for one evening and you put him in the hands of a baby-sitter—"

Before he could finish, Gabe's fist smashed into his jaw, sending the older man reeling backward. Casey, who'd only heard the end of the conversation as she and Ben approached, got between the two men. "Gabe, don't!" she shouted. "He's not worth it!"

"Better listen to the lady," Haynes warned, regaining his balance. "I don't have a problem with tossing your butt in jail—in fact, I rather like that idea."

"I'll just bet you would!"

"Gabe!" This was Casey.

"You've always been a hothead," Haynes said accusingly. "No wonder my Lisa was afraid of you!"

"You're lying!" Gabe yelled. "Lisa was never afraid of me!"

"Oh, but she was," Haynes snarled. "Why do you think she ran off to Paris?"

"You sent her there—supposedly to recover after B.J. died."

"You've told that story for so many years, you're starting to believe it yourself, aren't you, boy?" The other man chuckled with mock amusement.

"That's what Lisa told me."

"Well, what did you expect her to say? That she wanted to get away from you because you were a bomb about to go off?" he asked.

"This is ridiculous!" Casey intervened, annoyed by the discussion of Gabe's ex-wife. "Three men are trapped under that—rubble—and all you two have to argue about is whether or not Lisa was living in fear!" Motioning to her cameraman, she stalked off in anger.

Gabe stared after her, surprised by her outburst. Where, he wondered, did that come from?

Ignoring Haynes's continuing tirade, he took off after her.


"This is Casey Tucker at the site of the future Haynes Towers, where a portion of the new skyscraper under construction has collapsed, trapping the construction foreman, Mario Rizzo, and two of his men, George Miller and Sam Harris, beneath the tons of steel and concrete." In front of the camera, Casey was focused and totally professional. She did not allow herself to look at Gabe, who was standing on the sidelines, watching her live feed. Nor did she allow her face to betray the pain and anger she felt at him for still being so preoccupied with his ex-wife with all that was happening around them—to them.

"As you can see," she continued, "rescue workers are already at the site, attempting to reach the men, to determine if they are still alive."

"Did she say Mario Rizzo?" Delbert asked as he joined Gabe on the sidelines.

Gabe nodded. "Yeah, why?"

"I knew a Mario Rizzo," Delbert told him. "Years ago, in Florida. We were young, just kids, really."

"My father did live in Florida for a while, just before he married my mother."

Delbert turned to Joey, who stood behind him. "Your father?"

Joey nodded. "Mario Rizzo's my dad."

"I don't know that this is the same Mario Rizzo, but—" Delbert began.

"Well, my dad did live in Florida for a while—a few years, I think, and he did work on a fishing boat," Joey said, remembering. "And he talked a lot about his two buddies, Juan and Hokey—"

"Hokey was my nickname back then!" Delbert declared. "Then this Mario is my Mario—" His joy was cut short by the reality surrounding them. "Mario..."

"Wait a minute!" Joey said suddenly as the realization hit him. "You said you knew Juan down in Florida, too?"

Delbert nodded.

"Then Juan—Tootie's brother, Juan—is the guy you two were pals with down there."

"Well—yeah."

Casey concluded her live feed and spoke briefly to the cameraman, who turned to the rescue workers digging frantically at the corner of the collapsed building and continued to videotape the operation. Casey joined Gabe.

"Well, did you and your father-in-law get finished debating whether or not Lisa was really afraid of you?" she asked irritably.

"What's with you?" Gabe asked, not sure he understood. "Why are you so angry?"

"Angry? I'm not angry."

"Sure, you're not."

"All right, what if I were?" she asked. "Did it ever occur to you that you haven't let go of your past?"

"Hold it! Where is this all coming from? Who said I haven't resolved my feelings on my marriage?"

"Nobody said! It shows, every time she's the topic of conversation, Gabe—you're still in love with her!"

She started to walk away, but Gabe grabbed her arm. "For the record, I am *not* still in love with my ex-wife," he growled. "I've already told you that."

"At the risk of sounding cliché, actions speak louder than words," she snapped. "Now, if you don't mind, I'd like to see if Juan's found a way out yet—Marie's going to have that baby very soon, at the rate her labor's progressing."

Gabe followed her. He couldn't believe it. She was actually jealous!

"Joey... where's Joey?" Marie gasped, gripped by yet another contraction.

"He'll be back," Juan assured her. "He went only to see if there was someone at the site who could help us find a way out of here."

Casey jumped into the cab beside Marie. "I was hoping you two would be gone to the hospital by now."

"I'm beginning to wonder if we will ever get out of here," Juan said, trying not to let Marie know how worried he really was. "Maybe by the time this little one is ready for school."

"Oh, please, Juan—do not even joke about such things!" Marie wailed.

"How far apart are the contractions now?" Casey wanted to know.

"Less than five minutes—I think," said Marie.

Casey nervously looked at Juan, who swallowed a lump in his throat.

"How's she doing?" Gabe asked as he got into the cab.

"So far, so good," Juan told him, "but not for long, I don't think."

Casey didn't look up.

"I meant what I said," he told her.

"It's not important."

"Isn't it?"

"No."

"I love *you*, Case," he said then.

Before she could respond, Marie was overcome by yet another contraction. "This one is worse than the others," Marie cried, clutching Casey's hand fiercely.

"Juan, we've got to get out of here," Casey said, "or we have to deliver this baby!"

Juan's eyes rolled skyward as he made the sign of the cross. *"¡Dios!"* he gasped.

"You're a taxi driver—you've never delivered a baby?" Casey demanded.

"This is only my first week on the job," he pointed out. "I am supposed to know?"

"It would have made this a whole lot easier."

Gabe took over then. "Juan, go to that diner across the street and ask for some towels and some warm water. And I'll need a pair of scissors," he said.

"I have scissors." Casey dug into her bag to find them.

"Those look new," he commented as she handed them over. "Good."

"They still have to be sterilized," she said.

"Everything has to be sterilized."

"Where's Joey?" Casey asked then.

"Trying to help his father," Gabe said as he opened the back door and helped Marie into a better position for giving birth.

"I hope he gets back to see his baby born," Casey said sadly.

"When he found out it was his father who is trapped, with all that's been wrong between them, I think he was afraid he'd never have the chance to patch things up if he didn't go to him now. He also knows Marie has us to take care of her. And he'd be useless to us as nervous as he's been. I'm just as glad he's not here at the moment." He attempted to comfort Marie.

"Joey..." Marie moaned.

"Soon, Marie. He'll be back soon."

"Joey, he has always been regretful that he and his family were at odds," Marie said in a low, strained voice. "He would not admit it, of course, but it hurt him deeply. I think perhaps he will never get the chance to set things right now."

"Let's hope that's not going to be the case," said Casey.

"I do hope it is not, because I do not think Joey will be able to live with it," Marie told her. She let out a wail as yet another contraction overtook her.

"They're coming more frequently now—where's Juan with the towels?" Gabe asked, frustrated.

Juan was running when he returned to the car. "Did you hear?" he asked excitedly.

"Hear what?" Casey asked as Gabe took the towels and hot water from him.

"They got them! They got the men out!"

"Are they all right?" Casey asked.

"Yes, yes, they are all all right!" Juan said, elated. "They will take them to the hospital, of course, but they say they are not seriously harmed."

"It is a miracle," Marie said.

Gabe smiled down at her. "Yes, it is."

Then he looked up at Casey.


Juan went to see if he could get an ambulance to take Marie, and returned with Joey. "They are on their way," he announced as Joey went to his wife.

"I think they're going to be too late," Gabe said, shaking his head.

"The baby's coming now?" Joey asked, suddenly alarmed.

Gabe nodded. "Push, Marie—push!"

She let out a scream as she bore down, attempting to force the baby through. "Joey—hold my hand!" she cried.

Joey reached out and grasped both her hands. "I'm sorry I wasn't here—"

She tried to shake her head. "It is all right," she told him. "You saw your papa?"

"Yeah," he said, smiling. "He's okay. He'll be here in a minute."

"Here?" Casey asked. "But I thought they were taking them to the hospital."

"The other two, yeah—but Dad is fine, not a scratch on him," Joey said. "It did throw the fear of God into him, though—he was actually happy to see me!"

"One more time, Marie," Gabe urged. "Push—now!"

In what seemed like the blink of an eye, the baby emerged, red and wailing. "It's a girl," Gabe proclaimed.

Juan looked at his watch. "It's 12:15 a.m.," he said. "A Christmas baby!"

"We were so sure it would be a boy," Joey said, looking in wonder as Gabe cut the umbilical cord and started to clean up the baby.

"Disappointed?" Casey asked.

"No way!" he insisted. "It's just that we were so sure it would be a boy, we didn't even pick a girl's name."

"I have a suggestion," Casey offered.

"What would you call her?"

Casey smiled, but her eyes were on Gabe. "She was born on Christmas morning. How about Noelle?"

## Chapter Twelve

Casey watched as Marie and her newborn daughter were taken out of the ambulance and into the hospital's emergency room, with Joey following closely behind. As she started to go inside, too, a car pulled up and a man got out, exclaiming, "I'm a grandfather! I'm a grandfather!"

Mario Rizzo ran for the entrance, beaming, and Casey smiled, warmed by the man's change of heart toward his son and daughter-in-law. Gabe was right. Christmas was indeed a time for miracles.

Gabe. She turned back to the ambulance. Gabe was talking to the driver. Seeing her, he ended the conversation and joined her. "This must be all in a day's work for you," he said lightly.

She gave a weak laugh. "Hardly," she said as they started into the hospital. "I've been in the middle of a lot of action, but I've never seen a baby delivered before—on the job or off."

He stopped at the information desk to find out where Marie had been taken. "Third floor maternity," he told Casey, leading her down the hall to a bank of elevators. He stepped aside so she could enter, then followed closely behind, pushing the appropriate button. "Was that Mario Rizzo I saw coming in when I was talking to the ambulance driver?" he asked as the car began its slow ascent.

Casey nodded. "A brush with death does wonders for a man's perspective," she said.

"Not to mention a new grandchild," Gabe agreed.

The neonatal nursery was near the elevators, and they spotted Joey and his father at the window, admiring Noelle. "Not a proud daddy, are you?" Gabe chided Joey as he and Casey joined them.

"How could I not be proud?" Joey asked. "She's an angel, a real angel!"

"How's Marie?" Casey wanted to know.

"Marie's doin' great—now," Joey answered. "She's down the hall, room 305."

Casey nodded. "I'd like to look in on her before I go," she said.

"Go?" Gabe looked surprised.

"I have some unfinished business to take care of, remember?"

He gave her a quizzical look.

"Delbert. We *were* on our way to check out that lead on Cathy when we were, uh, unavoidably detained," she reminded him. "I think everything that can be done has been done here," she went on, "so I'm going to get my news truck and go find Del. With all that happened, he apparently got separated from us."

"Did he go back to the shelter?" Gabe asked.

"I doubt it."

"You don't think he went looking for Cathy on his own?"

"He has the address, the name of my contact."

Gabe remembered all too well what had happened the last time Casey had gone off chasing a lead. "We'd better find him as soon as possible."

The streets were dark and foreboding, like something in a B-detective movie. A fog was rolling in. There was little in the way of traffic, pedestrian or otherwise. Ben parked the station van on a side street and waited while Casey and Gabe set out on foot to find Delbert. "If anything goes wrong,"

Casey instructed, "call for help on the police radio."

"Will do," he promised.

They found the building with no problem, but no sign of Delbert. "See if you can find him," Casey said, handing him a tire iron. "I'll look for Cathy."

"What's this for?" Gabe asked, looking at the tire iron.

"Protection," she told him. "Look around, Gabe. This isn't exactly midtown."

"I'm not going to use this—"

"You might be surprised what you'll use if your life is on the line."

"Casey—"

"No time now, Wheeler. Go find Del."

Before he could stop her, she was headed into the building she'd been told to go to to find Cathy Vincent.

Sometimes he thought finding Cathy was as important to Casey as it was to Delbert.

He set off down the street, clutching the tire iron with great ambivalence. He didn't like this, didn't like it at all—but she was right, this wasn't such a great neighborhood.

Better safe than sorry, he thought.

He searched for what seemed like an eternity but was actually about half an hour. He was about to turn back when he saw a man across the street who looked like Delbert.

"Hey, Del!" he called out.

The man turned around . . .

"I'll tell you what I told the old geezer—there ain't no Cathy here!" The woman addressing Casey was small, bone-thin and unkempt looking, with stringy brown hair.

"Let me show you a picture of her." Casey stalled, craning her neck in a vain attempt to look over her head into the untidy apartment. Though there was nothing to indicate that there was anyone else in the apartment, she still had the feeling the woman was lying through her stained teeth.

"I ain't lookin' at no picture," she snapped crossly. "There ain't no Cathy here and I got better things to do than keep tellin' you there ain't!" She started to slam the door in her face, but Casey stopped her.

"I was told she was here."

"Well, whoever told you that was lyin'!" she growled.

"Vicky, what's goin' on?"

At the sound of the young female voice coming from the stairway, they both turned. The girl who had spoken couldn't have been more than eighteen—it was hard to tell because she was wearing so much makeup. She was dressed in a tight black barmaid's uniform under a cheap fake fur coat.

"Cathy Vincent?" Casey asked.

The girl turned on her high heels and ran.

"I went to that address—the one Casey's contact gave her—but the mean woman there said there was no girl living there, that she lived there alone," Delbert told Gabe as they headed back down the street.

"She could have been lying, Del," Gabe said pointedly. "If Cathy doesn't want to be found—and especially if she's fallen in with the wrong kind of people—this is to be expected."

"You think the woman was lying, then."

"I think there's a very good possibility."

"Then Cathy could be with some bad people," Delbert concluded. "I hope she hasn't—" He couldn't say the words; Gabe knew what he was thinking.

*"Cathy!"*

Both men looked in the direction of the woman's voice. Gabe saw the younger woman running into the street, with Casey following closely behind. "Cathy, wait!" she called out again as she gained on the girl.

"Cathy!" Delbert cried out, racing forward.

Gabe sprinted ahead of the older man, trying to head the girl off before she could get to a subway or a bus stop and make her getaway. He cut down a dark alley, hopped a fence and came out in the street in front of the fleeing girl.

"Cathy, stop!" he ordered.

She came to a screeching halt. "Please, let me go...please!" she begged, sobbing.

"We've been looking for you for so long," he gasped, trying to catch his breath.

"I don't want to go back there." She started crying. "Please don't make me go back."

"Cathy!"

The girl turned as Delbert approached. She looked at him as if she thought she knew who he was but wasn't quite sure. Casey caught up with them. "Cathy—this is your grandfather." She introduced them.


"You were already gone by the time I got back," Delbert told Cathy in the van, on the way back to the Guardian Angel Shelter. "I've been looking for you ever since."

"I had to get away," the girl said, recalling the incident. "I couldn't stay there—not in that house, not in that town. Not after Mama died."

"I wish I'd been there when you needed me, honey," Delbert said, putting an arm around her protectively.

In the front seat, Casey sat next to Gabe, wrapped in silence. She was thinking of her own family, lost to her forever. She envied Cathy the grandfather who'd fought so hard to find her, to give her a family life again.

If only she could have had that chance.

"I'll bet I know what you're thinking," Gabe said.

She managed a tired smile. "Am I that transparent?" Casey asked.

He smiled. "Pretty much so."

"I can't go back, I know that," she said, "but there are times...I just can't help wondering about what might have been."

"I know the feeling."

She looked at him. "Yes . . . you would."

"It's been five years, and I still miss B.J."

"I know." She took his hand, giving it a little squeeze. "But you have another chance."

"Yeah."

"Have you talked to Tim about it yet?" she asked.

He shook his head. "I was about to, when you showed up. I told him we'd talk when I came back," he reflected.

"Not getting cold feet, are you?"

"Not at all." He drew her closer. "As a matter of fact, I've been making some very definite plans for the future."


"Tim, I have a private investigator looking for your mother," Gabe told the boy after a delicious Christmas breakfast.

Tim frowned. "You won't find her. She doesn't want to be found."

"What makes you say that?" Tim had never been willing to talk much about his mother before, so his statement came as a surprise to Gabe.

"She's probably in California by now."

"Is that where she told you she was going?"

"She never told me anything," Tim answered. "She just talked about it a lot. She had a lot of magazines with stuff on California—read them a lot."

"That's where we'll look, then," Gabe told him.

"Why do we have to look for her at all?" the boy wanted to know.

"Don't you want to find her?"

"No. She didn't want me then—I don't want her now." There was bitterness—and sadness—in his voice.

"Well, we *have* to find her and bring her back here—at least for a little while," Gabe told him.

"What for?"

Gabe smiled. "Unless you have some objection, I'd like to become more than your legal guardian—I want to adopt you, if possible," he said.

Tim's eyes widened. "Adopt me?"

"Yeah—that is, if you want me to."

"You bet I do!" The boy flung his arms around Gabe's neck. "When I first came here to live, I used to wish that you were my dad, my real dad, and that I had a mom who loved me, too, and we had a great life together." He was beginning to cry.

Gabe's eyes were misty, too. "I'm working on it, son," he said softly. "I'm working on it."


"I watch it every year."

"I haven't seen it since I was a little girl."

Gabe had stopped at the video store on his way to Casey's apartment and rented the 1938 film version of Charles Dickens's *A Christmas Carol*. He'd also brought all the makings of a proper Christmas dinner: turkey, stuffing, yams, cranberries, hot rolls and pumpkin pie with whipped cream.

It was the best Christmas Casey had had in years. For the first time since the night of the fire, she was free of the past.

"I thought you'd bring Tim with you," Casey said as she snuggled against him on the couch.

Gabe shook his head. "I'm going to pick him up in a little while, and the three of us can have a family holiday. But now, I thought you and I should have some time alone ."

"Oh?" She looked up at him questioningly. "Sounds serious."

"I think we need to talk."

"About what?"

"For starters, about how you feel right now, after all we went through last night."

She gave him a puzzled look.

"I suspect the old wounds were opened wide last night, especially when we found Cathy," he said honestly.

"I dealt with it," she insisted.

"I'm sure you did," he said. "The question is, how do you feel right now?"

"About what?"

"About getting on with your life," he said. "About making a fresh start."

"I think I can do that now."

"Think? You're not sure?"

She shrugged. "Who knows about the future?" she asked. "I'm just taking it one day at a time."

"I see. Not making any long-range plans yet?"

She sat up again. "What is this?" she asked. "Why all the questions?"

"Just trying to figure out where your head is right now," he assured her.

"Well, thanks to you," she began, "my head is doing quite nicely, thank you very much. I don't expect the healing process to be completed overnight, but I think I've gotten off to a good start."

"I hope so."

"Have you talked to Tim yet—have you told him?" Casey asked.

He nodded. "Just a few hours ago."

"How'd he react?"

"He was upset at first," Gabe said, recalling the conversation.

"Upset?"

"I told him I was going to have to locate his mother," Gabe said. "That went over big."

"You didn't tell him *why* you had to bring her back here?" Casey was surprised.

"I'm afraid I stuck my foot in it," he admitted. "I could tell one thing for sure, though. He doesn't want her back—not now, at least."

"And she's not going to come back sometime in the future and want him back?" Casey worried aloud.

"I seriously doubt that, given the way she just dumped him at the Guardian Angel."

"So how does he feel about having you as his new father?" she asked.

"He told me he'd had a secret wish since he came to the shelter that I could be his father."

"He must really love you," Casey said, smiling. On the screen, old Scrooge was getting his from the Ghost of Christmas Past.

"It's mutual, believe me."

"I've known that for some time now."

"Tim told me something else when we were talking," Gabe said then. "Seems having me as his father was only part of his fantasy."

"Oh? There's more?"

"Definitely. In this fantasy he had a new mother, too."

"I see. Anyone we know?"

"She wasn't too clear in the dream—but I managed to clarify her face for him." He paused. "It was you, Casey."

She looked up at him, not sure she understood.

"Will you marry me, Casey?"

## Epilogue

As Casey stood gazing up at the Christmas tree in the shelter's living room, it filled her heart with a joy that sight hadn't brought her since she was a child. A joy nothing had given her in a very long time.

"Merry Christmas, sweetheart," Gabe said softly as he put his arm around her, drawing her close.

"It is, isn't it? Is Tim still asleep?" she asked.

"Snoring happily." He kissed the top of her head.

"I'd forgotten what a truly merry Christmas was like," she admitted. "I never believed it would be merry for me, ever again. I bet Tim felt the same way."

He looked up at the tree. "Well, they do say Christmas is a time for miracles," he reminded her.

"It sure is," she agreed. "Any word from the hospital?"

"Yeah—Wendy talked to Joey. Mother and baby are perfect, to quote the proud daddy."

"Are their families there with them?" Casey wanted to know.

Gabe nodded. "All of them. Joey told Wendy it was like a double family reunion in the fathers' waiting room," he chuckled. "She said he'd never sounded happier."

"Why do I get the feeling Joey and Marie's days at the Guardian Angel are numbered?" Casey asked suspiciously.

"They're not coming back."

"Not at all?"

He shook his head. "Nope. Joey will come by to get their things, but for the moment he's staying with his parents. When Marie and the baby are released from the hospital, they'll be going to her family's place until Joey gets his first paycheck and they get their own place."

"Paycheck?"

"His dad plans to get a new job and will get Joey one, too. The powers that be will most likely shut Ed Haynes down."

"Good. The job he interviewed for at my station will always be open to him, but I understand that he'd rather work with his father. That's really wonderful."

"The Rizzos will land on their collective feet, no matter what. Joey's dad's got a sterling reputation in the business, he can go anywhere from there— and he's promised to take Joey with him, no matter where he ends up. And I think Joey really wants to work with his dad."

"Marie must be thrilled."

"I'm sure she is."

"What about Joey's dad, anyway? Can you believe how, in all that mess last night, he and Juan and Delbert managed to cross paths again after all those years?"

"Like I said, it's a time for miracles." He laughed. "Would you believe they want to have a reunion here every year?"

"Here in New York?"

"No—here, as in at the construction site."

Casey laughed, too. "I hope we don't have to reenact the events of last night on an annual basis."

Gabe made a face. "I don't know about everyone else, but I have serious doubts about Marie's willingness to cooperate," he confided with a smile. "With all the donations sent to the station for the shelter, we may be able to help a lot of other mothers-to-be who find themselves in the situation Marie was in."

"I guess Delbert will be leaving soon, too."

Gabe nodded. "He's got no reason to stay now."

"Somebody mention my name?"

They both turned. Delbert and Cathy were coming in, arms around each other. "We were wondering where you two had gotten to," Casey said, happy to see them.

"We walked to St. Patrick's Cathedral," Cathy said. "This is our first Christmas together, and we wanted it to be something special."

"I think it was that last night," Gabe said pointedly.

Cathy laughed. "It was definitely something I'll be able to tell my grandchildren about," she agreed.

"Grandchildren!" Delbert snorted. "Now I really feel old."

"Did you see Tootie when you came in?" Gabe asked then.

Delbert nodded. "She and Juan stopped back for a few minutes after their dinner out, and now they're headed for dessert. He promised her something special."

"Special?" Gabe asked.

Delbert elaborated. "A dessert she won't have to share with Tim!"

Gabe and Casey laughed. "That's special, all right," Gabe said.

"Tootie thought so, too," Cathy giggled. "I wish I had come here when I first got to New York. Everybody here is so caring."

"It's the Ghosts of Christmases Past, Present and Future," Casey confided. "They're the ones who really run this place."

"When will you two be leaving?" Gabe asked Delbert.

"Pretty soon, I think."

"Not too soon, I hope."

"Why? Is there some reason we need to stay?" Delbert looked suddenly concerned.

"A good one, we think," Gabe said, grinning broadly. "We would like to have the two of you— and Tim and Joey and Marie and Tootie and Juan at our wedding."

Outside, the church bells began to ring.

*     *     *     *     *

## MILLION DOLLAR SWEEPSTAKES (III)

No purchase necessary. To enter, follow the directions published. Method of entry may vary. For eligibility, entries must be received no later than March 31, 1996. No liability is assumed for printing errors, lost, late or misdirected entries. Odds of winning are determined by the number of eligible entries distributed and received. Prizewinners will be determined no later than June 30, 1996.

Sweepstakes open to residents of the U.S. (except Puerto Rico), Canada, Europe and Taiwan who are 18 years of age or older. All applicable laws and regulations apply. Sweepstakes offer void wherever prohibited by law. Values of all prizes are in U.S. currency. This sweepstakes is presented by Torstar Corp., its subsidiaries and affiliates, in conjunction with book, merchandise and/or product offerings. For a copy of the Official Rules governing this sweepstakes offer, send a self-addressed, stamped envelope (WA residents need not affix return postage) to: MILLION DOLLAR SWEEPSTAKES (III) Rules, P.O. Box 4573, Blair, NE 68009, USA.

SWP-S1294

## HE'S MORE THAN A MAN, HE'S ONE OF OUR

**Fabulous Fathers**

### IDEAL DAD
### Elizabeth August

Eight-year-old Jeremy Galvin knew Murdock Parnell would make the perfect dad. Now it was up to Murdock to persuade Jeremy's mom, Irene, that he was the ideal husband for her.

*Ideal Dad,* available in January, is the third book in Elizabeth August's bestselling series, WHERE THE HEART IS.

Look for *Ideal Dad* by Elizabeth August—available in January.

### Fall in love with our Fabulous Fathers!

**Silhouette**
## ROMANCE™

FF195

**Those Harris boys are back in book three of...**

WEDDING WAGER

**by Sandra Steffen**

Three sexy, single brothers bet they'll never say "I do."
But the Harris boys are about to discover their vows of bachelor-
hood don't stand a chance against the forces of love!

You met Mitch in BACHELOR DADDY #1028 (8/94) and Kyle in
BACHELOR AT THE WEDDING #1045 (11/94). Now it's time for
brother Taylor to take the marriage plunge in—

EXPECTANT BACHELOR #1056 (1/95): When Gina Jenson sets
out to seduce the handsome Taylor, he's in for the surprise of his
life. Because Gina wants him to father her child!

# SILHOUETTE... Where Passion Lives

Don't miss these Silhouette favorites by some of our most distinguished authors! And now you can receive a discount by ordering two or more titles!

| | | | |
|---|---|---|---|
| SD#05786 | QUICKSAND by Jennifer Greene | $2.89 | ☐ |
| SD#05795 | DEREK by Leslie Guccione | $2.99 | ☐ |
| SD#05818 | NOT JUST ANOTHER PERFECT WIFE by Robin Elliott | $2.99 | ☐ |
| IM#07505 | HELL ON WHEELS by Naomi Horton | $3.50 | ☐ |
| IM#07514 | FIRE ON THE MOUNTAIN by Marion Smith Collins | $3.50 | ☐ |
| IM#07559 | KEEPER by Patricia Gardner Evans | $3.50 | ☐ |
| SSE#09879 | LOVING AND GIVING by Gina Ferris | $3.50 | ☐ |
| SSE#09892 | BABY IN THE MIDDLE by Marie Ferrarella | $3.50 U.S. <br> $3.99 CAN. | ☐ <br> ☐ |
| SSE#09902 | SEDUCED BY INNOCENCE by Lucy Gordon | $3.50 U.S. <br> $3.99 CAN. | ☐ <br> ☐ |
| SR#08952 | INSTANT FATHER by Lucy Gordon | $2.75 | ☐ |
| SR#08984 | AUNT CONNIE'S WEDDING by Marie Ferrarella | $2.75 | ☐ |
| SR#08990 | JILTED by Joleen Daniels | $2.75 | ☐ |

(limited quantities available on certain titles)

| | |
|---|---|
| AMOUNT | $_____ |
| DEDUCT: 10% DISCOUNT FOR 2+ BOOKS | $_____ |
| POSTAGE & HANDLING <br> ($1.00 for one book, 50¢ for each additional) | $_____ |
| APPLICABLE TAXES* | $_____ |
| TOTAL PAYABLE | $_____ |
| (check or money order—please do not send cash) | |

To order, complete this form and send it, along with a check or money order for the total above, payable to Silhouette Books, to: **In the U.S.:** 3010 Walden Avenue, P.O. Box 9077, Buffalo, NY 14269-9077; **In Canada:** P.O. Box 636, Fort Erie, Ontario, L2A 5X3.

Name:_____

Address: _____ City:_____

State/Prov.:_____ Zip/Postal Code:_____

*New York residents remit applicable sales taxes.
Canadian residents remit applicable GST and provincial taxes.                    SBACK-DF

Silhouette®